Tales of the Border

James Hall

LITERATURE HOUSE / GREGG PRESS
Upper Saddle River, N. J.

Republished in 1970 by
LITERATURE HOUSE
an imprint of The Gregg Press
121 Pleasant Avenue
Upper Saddle River, N. J. 07458

Standard Book Number—8398-0756-2
Library of Congress Card—74-104471

Printed in United States of America

TALES OF THE BORDER.

BY JAMES HALL,

Author of "Legends of the West," &c. &c.

PHILADELPHIA:

HARRISON HALL, NO. 47, SOUTH THIRD STREET.

1835.

CONTENTS.

PREFACE.

A few of the following Tales have been heretofore published in periodicals, but have not, it is supposed, been circulated to such an extent as to have been generally read; while the natural partiality which a writer feels towards his literary offspring has induced the author to wish to preserve them in a form less perishable than that in which they first appeared. The larger portion, however, of this volume is now presented for the first time to the public.

Although the garb of fiction has been assumed, as that which would afford the greatest freedom of description, the incidents which are related in these and other tales of the author are mostly such as have actually occurred; and he has only exercised his own

invention in framing the plots, so as to bring
together, in one sketch, the adventures which
may not have occurred in the connection in
which he has chosen to place them, or which
may have happened to different individuals.
In the descriptions of scenery he has not, in
any instance, intentionally departed from
nature, or exercised his own fancy in the
creation of a landscape, or in the exaggera-
tion of the features which he has attempted
to draw; and if the fidelity of his pictures
shall not be recognised by those who have
traveled over the same ground, the deficien-
cy will have resulted in the badness of the
execution, and not in any intentional devia-
tion from the originals.

In two of the tales, which occupy the
largest space in the volume, the author has
had an object in view, which will be readily
understood by those who are conversant
with American history, and especially by
those whose sympathies have been strongly
enlisted in behalf of the aborigines of our

country. Few are ignorant of the existence of that mutual antipathy which has drawn a broad line of separation between the white and red races, and kept alive a feud as deadly as it has been interminable. Yet all are not so well acquainted with the causes of that unhappy animosity, nor with the numberless irritating circumstances by which the passions of each party have been excited, and a jealousy so deplorable handed down from generation to generation. We have selected a few of those facts, such as most commonly occur, and have given them with little embellishment, and, we hope, without partiality.

The preparation of these sketches have cost the author but little labour; they are plain recitals of the traditions collected by other travellers upon our border, or of the legends which have amused his own hours while sitting by the hospitable fireside of the western farmer. Their brevity will probably secure them a perusal, in common with the

similar productions of the press. Should
any read them with instruction, the author
will be satisfied; should the critic pass them
over without censure, he will esteem himself
fortunate.

THE PIONEER.

I was travelling a few years ago, in the northern part of Illinois, where the settlements, now thinly scattered, were but just commenced. A few hardy men, chiefly hunters, had pushed themselves forward in advance of the main body of emigrants, who were rapidly but quietly taking possession of the fertile plains of that beautiful state; and their cabins were so thinly scattered along the wide frontier, that the traveller rode many miles, and often a whole day together, without seeing the habitation of a human being. I had passed beyond the boundaries of social and civil subordination, and was no longer within the precincts of any organised country. I saw the camp of the Indian, or met the solitary hunter, wandering about with his rifle and his dog, in the full enjoyment of that independence, and freedom from

2

all restraints, so highly prized by this class of our countrymen. Sometimes I came to a single log hut, standing alone in the wilderness, far removed from the habitations of other white men, on a delightful spot, surrounded by so many attractive and resplendent beauties of landscape, that a prince might have selected it as his residence ; and again I found a little settlement, where a few families, far from all other civilised communities, enjoyed some of the comforts of society among themselves, and lived in a state approaching that of the social condition.

But whether I met the tawny native of the forest, or the wild pioneer of my own race, I felt equally secure from violence. I found them always inoffensive, and usually hospitable. That state of continual warfare, which marked the first settlements upon the shores of the Ohio, had ceased to exist. The spirit of the red man was broken by repeated defeat. He had become accustomed to encroachment, and had learned to submit to that which he could not prevent. However deeply he might feel the sense of injury, and however fiercely the fires of revenge might burn within his bosom, too many lessons of severe experience had taught him to restrain his passions. Bitter experience had inculcated the lesson, that every blow struck at the white man recoiled with ten-fold energy upon himself.

I found the pioneers a rude but a kind people. The wretched hovels, built of rough logs, so carelessly joined together as to afford but a partial protection from the storm, afforded a welcome shelter, when compared with the alternative of *"camping out,"* which I had been obliged to adopt more frequently than was agreeable. Their tables displayed little variety, but they were spread with a cheerful cordiality that was delightful to the weary traveller. There were venison, poultry, rich milk, and excellent bread, in abundance. There was honey too, for those that liked it, fresh and fragrant from the cell of the wild bee. But the smile of the hostess was that which pleased me most ; her hospitable reception of the tired stranger—the alertness with which she prepared the meal—her attention to his wants—the sympathy she expressed for any misadventure that had befallen him, and the confidence with which she tendered the services of "her man," when it happened that the more slowly spoken host faltered in the performance of any of the rites of hospitality ;—all these, while they afforded the evidence of a noble trait of nationality, which I recognised with pride as a western American, reminded me also of the delicacy and quickness of perception with which a woman recognises the wants of him who "has no mother to bring him milk, no wife to grind his corn."

I halted once upon the "Starved Rock," a spot rendered memorable by a most tragic legend which has been handed down in tradition. It is a stupendous mass of insulated rock, standing upon the brink of the Illinois river, whose waters wash its base. Viewed from this side, it is seen to rise perpendicularly, like the ramparts of a tall castle, frowning over the still surface of that beautiful stream, and commanding an extensive prospect of low, but richly adorned, and quiet, and lovely shores. Passing round, the bulwark of rock is found to be equally precipitous and inaccessible on either side, until the traveller reaches the rear, where a narrow ledge is found to slope off from the summit towards the plain, affording the only means of access to this natural fortress. Here a small tribe of Indians, who had been defeated by their enemies, are said to have taken refuge with their wives and children. The victorious party surrounded the rock, and cut off the wretched garrison from all possibility of retreat, and from every means of subsistence. The siege was pressed with merciless rigour, and the defence maintained with undaunted obstinacy—exhibiting, on either side, those remarkable traits of savage character: on the one, the insatiable and ever vigilant thirst for vengeance; on the other, unconquerable endurance of suffering. The position is so inaccessible, that any attempt to carry it by assault was wholly impracticable, and the dreadful expedient was adopted of reducing it by starvation—an expedient which was rendered inevitably and rapidly successful, by the circumstance that the summit of the rock afforded no water, and that the besieged party had laid in no supply of provisions.

It is shocking to reflect on such warfare. There is nothing in it of the pomp, or pride, or circumstance, which often deceive us into an admiration of deeds of violence. In reading of the stern conflict of gallant men who meet in battle, our feelings are enlisted by the generosity which exposes life for life. The "plumed troops, and the big wars," stir up the soul to a momentary forgetfulness of the vices they engender, and the wretchedness they produce, though we cannot agree with the poet, that they "make ambition virtue." We admire the genius which plans, and the talent that executes, a successful stratagem, and pay the homage of our respect to any bright development of military science. Courage always wins applause; we cannot withhold our approbation from a daring act, even though the motive be wrong. But bravery on a fair field, and in a good cause, becomes heroism, and warms the heart into an enthusiastic admiration. How different from all this, and from all that constitutes the chivalry of warfare, and how like the cold-blooded sordidness of a deliberate murder, was that savage act of starving to death a

2*

whole tribe,—the warriors, the aged, the females, and the children! And such, in fact, became the fate of that unhappy remnant of a nation which had once possessed the sovereignty over these beautiful plains, and had hunted, and fought, and sat in council, in all the pride of an independent people. The pangs of hunger and thirst pressed them, but they maintained their post with obstinate courage, determined rather to die of exhaustion, than to afford their enemies the triumph of killing them in battle or exposing them at the stake. Every stratagem which they attempted was discovered and defeated. When they endeavoured to procure water in the night, by lowering vessels attached to long cords into the river, the vigilant besiegers detected the design, and placed a guard in canoes to prevent its execution. They all perished—one, and only one, excepted. The last surviving warriors defended the entrance so well, that the enemy could neither enter nor discover the fatal progress of the work of death ; and when, at last, all show of resistance having ceased, and all signs of life disappeared, the victors ventured cautiously to approach, they found but one survivor—a squaw, whom they adopted into their own tribe, and who was yet living, at an advanced age, when the first white men penetrated into this region.

One morning, on resuming my journey, I found that my way led across a wide prairie. The road was a narrow foot-path, so indistinct as to be scarcely visible among the high grass. As I stood in the edge of a piece of woodland, and looked forward over the extensive plain, not the least appearance of forest could be seen—nothing but the grassy surface of the broad natural meadow, with here and there a lonely tree. It was in the spring of the year, and the verdure was exquisitely fresh and rich. The undulating plain, sloping and swelling into graceful elevations, was as remarkable for the beauty of its outline as for the resplendent brilliancy of its hues. But although the prairie was so attractive in appearance, there was something not pleasant in the idea of crossing it alone. The distance over it, to the nearest point of woodland, was thirty miles. There was, of course, neither a house nor any shelter by the way—nothing but the smooth plain, with its carpet of green richly adorned with an endless variety of flowers. To launch out alone on the wide and blooming desert, seemed like going singly to sea; and it was impossible to avoid feeling a sense of lonesomeness when I looked around, as far as the eye could reach, without seeing a human being or a habitation, and without the slightest probability of beholding either within the whole day. As I rode forth from the little cabin which had given me shelter through the night, I could not avoid looking back repeatedly at the grove which surrounded it, with a wistful.

ness like that of the mariner as he regards a slowly
receding shore. But the sun was rising in majestic lustre from the low distant horizon, shedding a
flood of light over the placid scene, and causing
the dew-drops that gemmed the grass to sparkle
like a silver tissue—and I spurred my steed forward with mingled sensations of delight and pensiveness.

I soon became convinced that the journey of this
day was likely to prove disagreeably eventful.
There had recently been some heavy falls of rain,
and the ravines which intersect the prairie, and
serve as drains, were full of water. Some of these
are broad, and many of them too deep to be crossed
when filled, without obliging the horse to swim;
and the banks are often so steep, that, before the
rider is aware of his danger, the horse plunges
forward headlong, throwing the unwary traveller
over his neck into the stream. I rode on, however, wading through pools and ravines, but happily
escaping accident, and meeting with no place sufficiently deep to try the skill of my steed in the
useful art of swimming, though the water often
bathed his sides, and sometimes reached nearly to
his back. Nor was this all—" misfortunes never
come single." The clouds began to pile themselves up in the west,—rolling upward from the
horizon portentously black. The signs were omi-
nous of a day of frequent and heavy showers. But

how could I help myself? On a prairie there is
no refuge from the fury of the storm, any more
than there is upon the ocean; and to warn a traveller that the rain is soon to fall, is about as prac-
tically useful to him as would be the inculcation of
that ancient canon of the church,—" No man may
marry his grandmother." I looked back at the
clouds, and then looked forward to a wetting. It
is vexatious to be caught thus. A shower-bath is
pleasant enough when taken voluntarily, but not
so when it must be received upon compulsion. To
be wet is no great misfortune, nor is there any
thing dangerous or melancholy in the occurrence.
But this only makes it the more provoking. If
there was any thing pathetic in the catastrophe of
a ducking, or any bravery to be evinced in bearing
the pitiless peltings of the storm, it might do. But
there is no sympathy for wet clothes, nor does a
man earn any tribute of respect for his patient endurance, when sitting like a nincompoop under the
outpourings of a thundergust. The whole affair
is undignified and in bad taste. Few things so
humble one's pride, and make one feel so utterly
insignificant, and so like a wet rag, as to be soaked
to the skin against our own consent.

It was thus that I felt on this unlucky day. The
clouds rolled on until the whole heavens became
overcast. That splendid sun which had risen so
joyously, and lighted up the landscape, and glad

dened the face of nature, was obscured, and heavy
shadows pervaded the plain. The clouds settled
down, until the low arch of suspended fluid appeared
to rest upon the prairie. I drew on my great coat.
A blast of wind swept past me—then the rain fell
in torrents upon my back, as if poured out from ten
thousand water buckets. What a dunce was I
to put on my over-coat, which only served as a
spunge to suck in the descending cataract, and load
me down with an accumulated weight. The rain
poured in streams from the eaves of my hat—it
beat upon my neck, and insinuated itself under my
clothes—it ran down into my boots, and filled them
until they overflowed. I felt cowed, crest-fallen,
hen-pecked—I compared myself to a drowned rat
—to a pelted incumbent of the pillory—to any
thing but an honest man, a republican, and a gentleman. I got vexed, and kicked my spurs into
my horse, who, instead of mending his pace, only
threw up his head indignantly, as if to reproach
me for the supplementary torture thus gratuitously
bestowed upon my companion in trouble. I re-
lented, drew in my rein, stopped short, and just sat
still and took it—and presently the rain stopped
also. It cannot rain always.

I drew a long breath, and looked around me, as
the war of the elements ceased. My saturated
garments hung shapelessly about my person, and
I had the cold comfort of knowing that there they

must continue to hang, and I to shiver under them, until all the particles of moisture should be carried away by the slow process of evaporation—for the rain had penetrated my saddle-bags and soaked my whole wardrobe. The clouds still looked watery, and were rolling up in heavy masses, portentous of new and repeated showers. If it would not have been unmanly, and unlucky too, I should have turned back, and regained the shelter of my last night's lodgings—but I was as wet as I could be, and—as General Washington said when he was sitting for his portrait—" in for a penny, in for a pound."

As I looked about me I perceived, at a great distance, a horseman approaching in my rear, and travelling in the same direction with myself. I determined to wait for him,—the more readily, as I had just arrived at the brink of a ravine which was broader and apparently deeper than any I had passed, and in which, in consequence of the recent shower, the water was rushing rapidly. Any company at such a time was better than none: I was willing to run the risk of being scalped by a Winnebago, talked out of my senses by a garrulous Kentuckian, or questioned to death by a travelling - Yankee, rather than ride any further alone.

As the traveller approached me and halted, with the courtesy usual in the country, I was struck with his appearance. From his countenance one

would have pronounced him to be a soldier, but his
garb was that of a methodist preacher. Dressed
in the coarse homespun fabric which is made, and
almost universally worn, in this region, there was
yet a dignity in the air and conduct of this stranger which was independent of apparel. His coarse
and sunburnt complexion was that of a person who
had been exposed to the elements from childhood.
It was not scorched and reddened by recent exposure, but regularly tanned and hardened, until its
texture would have bid defiance to the attacks of a
musquito, or any other insect or reptile of less
muscular powers than the rattlesnake. His features were composed, but the air of perfect calm
that rested upon them was that of reason and
reflection operating upon a vigorous mind, which
had once been violently excited by passion. There
could be no mistake in the expression of these
thin compressed lips, indicating unalterable resolution and sternness of purpose. The high relief,
and strong development of the muscles of the face,
evinced the long continued impulse of powerful
emotion. But the small gray eye was that which
most attracted attention. It was fierce, and bold,
yet subdued. Time and the elements had driven
the blood from the cheeks, but the eye retained
all the fire of youth. There was an intensity in
its glance which caused another eye to sink or turn
aside, rather than gaze at it directly; and this

was not in consequence of any thing sinister or repulsive in the expression, but because the power of vision seemed to be so concentrated and intense as to defy concealment. There was a vigilance, too, about that eye, as I had afterwards occasion to observe, which seemed never to sleep, and suffered nothing to escape its attention. Without at all disturbing the sedate demeanour of the body, and the nearly motionless position of the head—the eye, moving quietly and almost imperceptibly under the lid, watched all that passed around, while the ear caught the slightest sound with an acuteness which was extraordinary to one not accustomed to this perfect exercise of the faculty of attention.

In the wilderness, it is well understood that strangers who meet may address each other with frankness: it was soon discovered that we were travelling in the same direction, and agreed that we should go together. The stranger took the lead; and if I was at first struck with his appear- ance, I was now even more surprised at his perfect composure, under circumstances which were cer- tainly unpleasant, and perhaps dangerous. He rode into the ravine before us, as carelessly as if it had formed a part of the hard path, neither changed position nor countenance as his horse began to swim, managed the animal with the most perfect ease and expertness, and, on reaching the

3

opposite shore, continued to move quietly forward, without seeming to notice the splashing and puffing which it was costing me to effect the same operation.

As we rode on we found the earth saturated, and the surface of the plain flowing with water. Throughout the day the showers were frequent and heavy, gust after gust passed over us, each as furious as the last. We had to wade continually through pools, or to swim our horses through torrents. My companion minded none of these things, and I became astonished at the imperturbable gravity with which he encountered those difficulties, which had not only fatigued me nearly to death, but so worried my patience that I had grown nervous and irritable. On he plunged, through thick and thin, selecting the best paths and crossing places—guiding his horse with consummate skill—favouring the animal by avoiding obstacles, and taking all advantages which experience suggested,—yet pushing steadily on through impediments which, at first sight, seemed to me impassable. On such occasions he took the lead, as he did generally along the narrow path which we could only travel comfortably in single file; but, when the ground permitted, we rode abreast and engaged in conversation.

Towards evening we arrived at the brink of a small river, not wide, but brim-full, and whose

stream swept along impetuously, bearing logs and
the recently riven branches of trees upon its foaming bosom. The idea of swimming on the backs
of our tired horses, over such a torrent, was not to
be entertained; and I actually groaned aloud, in
despair, at the thought of being obliged to spend
the night upon its banks. But my companion,
without halting, observed calmly, that a more
favourable place for crossing might possibly be
found; and, turning his horse's head along the
brink of the river, began to trace its meanders.
Presently we came to a spot where a large tree
had fallen across, the roots adhering to one bank
while the top rested upon the other. My companion dismounted and began to strip his horse,
leaving nothing on him but the bridle, the reins of
which he fastened carefully over the animal's
head, and then leading him to the water, drove
him in. The horse, accustomed to such proceedings, stepped boldly into the flood, and, stemming
it with a heart of controversy, swam snorting to
the opposite shore, followed by my trusty steed.
We then gathered up our saddles, and other
"plunder," and mounting the trunk of the fallen
tree, crossed with little difficulty, caught our steeds
who were waiting patiently for us, threw on our
saddles, and proceeded.

It was night when we reached a cabin, where
we were hospitably entertained. Kindly as stran-

gers are always received in this region, I could
not but observe that the ecclesiastical character of
my companion excited, on this occasion, an unusual
assiduity of attention and homage of respect. The
people of our frontier are remarkable for the propriety of their conduct in this particular. However rude or careless their demeanour towards
others may sometimes be, a minister of the gospel
is always received at their houses with a mixture
of reverence and cordiality, which shows the
welcome given him to be as sincere as it is
liberal. They seem to feel unaffectedly grateful
for the labours of these devoted men in their
behalf, and to consider themselves honoured, as
well as obliged, by their visits. And none deserve
their gratitude and affection in a greater degree
than the preachers of that sect to which my companion belonged. They are the pioneers of religion. They go foremost in the great work of
spreading the gospel in the desolate places of our
country. Wherever the vagrant foot of the hunter
roams in pursuit of game—wherever the trader is
allured to push his canoe by the spirit of traffic—
wherever the settler strikes his axe into the tree,
or begins to break the fresh sod of the prairie, the
circuit-riders of this denomination are found min-
gling with the hardy tenants of the wilderness,
curbing their licentious spirit, and taming their
fierce passions into submission. They carry the

Bible to those, who, without their ministry, would only

"See God in clouds, or hear him in the wind."

They introduce ideas of social order, and civil restraint, where the injunctions of law cannot be heard, and its arm is not seen. And these things they do at the sacrifice of every domestic comfort, and at the risk of health and life. At all seasons, and in all weathers, they go fearlessly on; riding through trackless deserts, encamping in the open air, crossing rivers, and enduring the same hardships which beset the hunter in the pursuit of his toilsome calling, or the soldier in the path of victory.

These reflections occurred to my mind when I recalled the superiority over myself, young and vigorous as I thought I was, which my companion had shown in surmounting the difficulties of a border journey. As I saw him seated at the cheerful fireside of the woodsman, I was surprised to perceive how little he seemed affected by the fatigues of the day, how totally he appeared to forget them, and with what ease and earnestness he conversed with the family on serious topics suggested by himself. He sat with them as their equal and their friend. He enquired familiarly about their health, their crops, their cattle, and all their concerns—led them gradually to speak of

3*

their moral habits, and, finally, of their religious
opinions. As the time to retire approached, he
drew the sacred volume from his pocket, and proceeded to the performance of that service which
has always struck me as the most solemn and affecting of religious exercises—the worship of the
family—where those united by the tenderest ties
of affection kneel together before the throne of
grace, to render their humble tribute of thanks
for blessings received, and to invoke for each
other the continued protection of Heaven.

On the following morning we departed at the
dawn. I accompanied my new acquaintance several days, during which we experienced a variety
of adventures and hardships; and I had many
opportunities for observing the courage of my
companion, his perfect self-possession under every
vicissitude, and his skill in all the arts of the
backwoodsman. He was the most accomplished
woodsman that I have ever met. No danger
could daunt him, no obstacle impeded our way
which he had not some expedient to obviate or
avoid. He was never deceived as to the points of
the compass or the time of day. If our path
became dim, or seemed to wind away from the
proper direction, he struck off without hesitation
across the prairie, or through the forest, and
always reached the place which he sought with
unerring certainty. Community of peril and ad-

venture soon begets friendship, and our casual
acquaintance ripened speedily into intimacy. I
became struck with the conversational powers of
my companion; though habitually taciturn, he
sometimes grew social and communicative, and
then his language was energetic, his train of
thought original, and his figures bold and rheto-
rical. He seemed to have no acquaintance with
books, but had studied nature, and had stored his
mind with a fund of allusions drawn from her
ample volume. There was something mysterious
about him that excited my curiosity. His peace-
ful garb and holy calling were entirely inconsistent
with his military bearing, his keen jealous eye, his
intimate acquaintance with the artifices of the
hunter, and the wistful glances which I sometimes saw him throw at the rifles of the persons
we occasionally met. At last I ventured to suggest the impressions made upon my mind by these
seeming contradictions, and was gratified by a
frank relation of his history. It was minutely
detailed in the course of several conversations.
I cannot pretend to repeat his wild emphatic language, but will give the story as nearly as I can
in his own manner.

THE PIONEER'S TALE.

There are some events in my life, said my friend, to which I cannot look back without shuddering. Although time has cooled my feelings, and given a better tone to the decisions of my judgment, it has not destroyed the vividness of those impressions which were made upon my memory in childhood. They still present themselves with all the familiarity of recent transactions; and there are times when a peculiar combination of circumstances awakens them with a freshness that seems to partake more of reality than of recollection, and when I can hardly persuade myself that the same scenes are not again about to be acted over. Sometimes a particular state of the atmosphere, the position of the clouds, and the distribution of light and shade, give a character to the landscape which transports me back in a moment to the days of childhood, and pictures, in living truth upon my imagination, an event which occurred under such circumstances, as to have connected it indissolubly with those natural appearances. A sound has suddenly poured in a train of associations: the song of the bird in some distant tree, the hooting of an owl, the long dissonant bay of the wolf, borne on the still air when the moonlight reposed on the tops of the

trees, has awakened reminiscences which reach
back almost to infancy.

I have but an indistinct recollection of my father.
I have endeavoured to preserve the impression, for
there is a sacredness connected with his memory,
which renders it dear to my heart; but it is so
dim, and so shadowed over by other images, that
I know not whether it be the real impress made by
his kindness on my young nature, or the offspring
of fancy. He was one of the pioneers who came
to the forests of Kentucky, among the first adventurers to that scene of disastrous conflict. My
mother followed his footsteps to the wilderness,
bearing me, an infant, in her arms, resolved to
participate in the vicissitudes of his fortune, however precarious, and to brave all the dangers and
hardships of a border life, rather than endure the
greater pain of separation. Their cabin was
reared upon the shores of the Kentucky river, in
one of the most blooming valleys of that Eden,
which nature seems to have created in a moment
of prodigal generosity. They were happy; though
destitute of all that constitutes the felicity of the
larger portion of mankind. Without society, with
no luxuries, and with few of the comforts of civilised life, they were content in the society of each
other. My father was a bold and successful hunter;
he delighted to rove over those fertile plains,
whose magnificent forests, abounding in game, and

rich in beauty, were so alluring to every lover of
sylvan sport. Having selected an excellent tract
of land, from which he began to clear the trees,
he indulged, like others, in flattering anticipations
of the wealth and independence which would
crown his labours; when these broad lands should
become the seat of an industrious population, and
when Kentucky, then the paradise of hunters,
should be the garden of Western America. These
were not visionary dreams; though he and others
who indulged them did not live to behold their ac-
complishment, their descendants have seen them
abundantly fulfilled.

This spot was the birth-place of my sister. I
remember her too, with a fondness that no subsequent emotion has equalled or effaced. I cannot
forget her, for she was my only playmate. The
bitter moment when I realised the truth, that this
sweet child was separated from us, to be restored
no more in this world, caused a gush of anguish,
almost too strong for the tenderness of my young
affections, and left a wound which saddened my
spirits throughout the years of my early life.

Year after year rolled away, and my parents
continued in the wilderness, almost alone, and
exposed to continual danger. At first, the frequent alarms caused by the incursions of the
savages, and the many vicissitudes incident to
their situation, produced discontent, and they

would probably have returned to North Carolina,
had it not been for the shame of turning their
backs on danger, and leaving others exposed to
that which they would have avoided. But the
burthen gradually grew lighter, and their strength
to bear it increased. The little cabin appeared
more and more comfortable, because its inmates
became accustomed to its narrow dimensions, and
its meagre accommodations. It was their HOME;
it was the spot where they began to live for each
other, to enjoy the endearments of conjugal affection, and to accumulate the comforts of domestic
life around them; and every year brought some
addition to their little circle of enjoyments, and
added new links to the chain of agreeable associations, which at last rendered this retreat,
savage as it was, the dearest place to them on
earth. So my mother has told me; and I well
remember the glow of feeling with which she
spoke of those years, and of that spot which was
her first home in the wilderness.

She had to endure many sufferings; but they
were light when placed in the balance against
the pleasures that sweetened her existence. Her
husband cherished her with tenderness; and with
the shield of his affection around her, the clouds
of sorrow, though they might sadden her heart
for a moment, could not chill it with the withering blight which falls on those who are alone in

the world. In the labours of husbandry, they
toiled as others toil : their hopes were sometimes
disappointed—the frost blasted their grain, a
drought shortened their crops, the enemy ravaged
their fields, or drove away their cattle, and they
found themselves as poor as when they first began
the world. But they lived in a plentiful country ;
their neighbours, though few, were hospitable,
and they never knew want. The pangs of hunger—the deeper anguish of listening to the cries
of famishing children, are not among the evils
which infest the dwelling of the American bor-
derer. She had her hours of solitude ; when my
father was employed in wielding the axe, or
guiding the plough, with his loaded rifle at hand,
and his dog keeping watch, to prevent surprise
by the Indians, she pursued her appropriate
duties in silence and pensiveness at home. But
she was working for him, and this reflection supported her in his absence, until his return brought
an ample recompense for the temporary deprivation of his society. Those who reside in towns,
or in thickly settled neighbourhoods, cannot understand the full force of this language ; but
thousands of matrons are daily realising upon the
frontiers of our country,. that which I describe.
The young wife has left father and mother to
cleave unto her husband—she has abandoned the
parental roof, the home of childhood, the com-

panions of her infancy—the tenderness of a proud
father, the care of an experienced mother, are
hers no longer—she has left the circle of intimate
friends by whom she is known and appreciated—
and she has followed cheerfully, in the buoyancy
of hope and love, the footsteps of the husband of
her choice, to some spot beautifully embellished
by the hand of nature, where they anticipate all
the joys of Arcadian felicity. But their dwelling
stands alone, separated from all others by miles
of forest, or uninhabited prairie. All her affections are concentrated upon him who is her only
friend and sole companion; and that tie which
is ordinarily so sweet, so strong, and so indissolu-
ble, becomes more powerful by the absence of all
other objects of attachment or companionship.
The office of the husband assumes a tenderer
and holier character,—for he is the only adviser,
friend, and protector, of her who has forsaken all
for him. In his absence she sits alone, for the
time being a widowed and desolate creature. If
disease suddenly invade the dwelling there is no
friend nor neighbour at hand; if an accident
befal her infant, she has perhaps no messenger
to send for assistance; and in those early times,
in which the scenes that I relate occurred, there
was the continual terror of the savage, pressing
like the hideous monster of an unquiet dream,
upon the bosom of the wife, who, in the absence

4

of her husband, was terrified alike by his exposure to danger, and her own unprotected condition. Often did the young mother, of those days, hide her infant in some secret place, while she pursued her domestic labours.

My father, fearless himself, placed too little confidence in the reality of such perils; and although generally at home, suffered himself occasionally to be persuaded to join a hunt, or a war party. Sometimes a longer hunt than usual, or an accident, detained him from home all night, and then my mother passed the sleepless hours in listening to catch the sound which might announce his return, and dreading the moment when the stealthy footstep of the Indian might invade the sanctity of her dwelling. On such occasions, she would hide her sleeping infants, in some secret spot, not likely to be suspected, and then retire to her own bed, awaiting the result in anxious suspense. But the severest of all the trials of her fortitude came, when the pioneers were summoned to the field, and my father joined the parties of armed rangers, who drove the savages from our settlements, or pursued them to their own villages. Then it was, that day after day, and night after night, she watched, and wept, and prayed, and felt herself already bowed down in anticipation, under the hopeless grief of an imaginary widowhood.

At length the blow came. The storm, whose voice had often been heard at a distance, and which had thrown its lengthened shadow over our little dwelling, burst over us in the fulness of its destructive energy. One day my father had gone out to a piece of ground which he was clearing, not far from the house, accompanied by a few of the neighbouring men, who had assembled to assist him in rolling some large logs into heaps, for burning. My mother was employed in sewing, while my little sister and myself played on the floor. She heard the crack of a rifle, in the direction of the newly cleared ground, and as this was always a sound which excited interest in the mind of the wife of a pioneer, in those days of continual warfare, she hastily stepped to the door to listen. A single report did not necessarily imply danger, for the farmers always carried their rifles with them to the field of labour; and they might have fired at one of the wild animals with which the forest abounded. But another and another report followed in quick succession—and then the shrill war-whoop of the Indian—that terrific sound, which once heard, is never forgotten. The little party had been attacked by the savages. My mother rushed out of the house. Her first impulse was to hasten to the scene of action, to aid her husband with her feeble strength, or die by his side. But

the recollection of her children, and the conviction that she could render no service in the battle,
but might endanger the safety of her little ones
by abandoning the spot which was her post of
duty, restored her presence of mind ; and she
climbed to the top of a high fence, to catch, if
possible, a view of the combatants. The guns
continued to be discharged in rapid succession ;
she saw the smoke rising in thin columns from
each explosion, and settling in a dense cloud over
the field of conflict, and, under the dark shadow
of the edge of the forest, even the flashes were
visible. What a scene for a wife to witness!
The yells of the Indians were mingled with the
shouts of the white men—the screams of anguish,
and the horrible exclamations of revenge, were
borne together to the ear of the affrighted and
only spectator of this bloody drama.

In this moment of horror, the distracted mother
heard the piercing screams of one of her children,
and rushed instinctively to the house, expecting
to find that the savages had also approached in
that direction. My little sister had fallen into
the fire, and was severely burned. She snatched
up her child, began to tear the blazing clothes
away from it, and soon ascertained, that the
injury, though severe, was not dangerous. While
thus employed, she became conscious that the
war-whoop had died away, and the firing ceased,

What a moment for the wife and mother! What excruciating torments are inflicted upon the helpless dependents, and inoffensive companions of man, by his ambition, his fierce passions, and his reckless prodigality of life! The battle was over, and the slain were lying upon the field. She knew not certainly that any had fallen, but the probability was, that even if the white men were victorious, the triumph had been purchased by a heart-breaking loss to some unhappy wife, or wretched mother—perhaps to herself. But if the Indians had prevailed, how accumulated the horror of her situation! The tomahawk might even now be performing its brutal office in despatching the vanquished, or mutilating the dead, and in a few moments she might be compelled to witness the expiring agonies of her children!

She wept bitterly over her screaming infant, and almost blamed the unconscious child that detained her from rushing to her husband. Unable to restrain her impatience, she hastened to the door with the babe in her arms, and saw the little party of backwoods-men slowly returning. Why came they with such tardy steps—why thus closely crowded together—why did they halt so often? Alas! they bore one of their number a corpse in their arms! She ran to meet them. As she came near, the men laid down their bur-

4*

then under the shade of a large tree, and then
stood respectfully back—while my poor mother,
recognising her husband in the agonies of death,
threw herself on the ground beside him, and had
only time to attract one look from the dying man,
by her shriek of agony, ere his eyes were closed
for ever.

The remains of my father were buried near
the house, and my mother could not be prevailed
upon to quit the spot around which her affections
lingered. After spending a few weeks at the
house of a neighbour, who had kindly taken us
home during the confusion of the melancholy
event, she returned to her deserted cabin, having,
in the mean while, written to an unmarried brother in North Carolina to come to her. He
came and remained with us, carrying on the
business of our farm, and acting as a kind protector to us all.

From this period I date the commencement of
my recollections. I remember well the care-worn
figure and broken-hearted countenance of my mother. She was so bowed down under affliction
that her voice had acquired a tremulous tone,
which was very touching to those who knew the
cause, and especially to the few who participated
in her grief. The neighbours were kind to her;
they gathered her corn, looked after her affairs,
and provided for her until my uncle's arrival; and

continued ever afterwards to treat her with considerate attention. There are few who do not feel deep sympathy for the utter desolation of the widow's heart, and for the helpless wretchedness of her unprotected situation; nor do any people exhibit, in the indulgence of this natural feeling, a more manly benevolence than our backwoodsmen. Continually exposed to danger, and dependent on each other for a thousand charitable offices, which are always rendered without remuneration, they do not become callous to the misery of others, but learn to feel and act as if bound to those around them by the ties of fraternity. They visited my mother often; and the story of my father's death was repeated so frequently as to be deeply impressed upon my memory. In the higher circles of life, where a great degree of refinement is said to prevail, it is not customary, I believe, to converse with the parties interested upon those sad topics which deeply affect the heart, and throw a gloom over the family circle. In humble life it is different: the fountains of grief are familiarly approached and thrown open, and the bitter waters of affliction suffered to flow freely out. The heart relieves itself by these discussions, and, instead of brooding over its sorrows, gives them vent, and does better than adding imaginary ills to those which are real, by learning to consider the subject in the same practical light in which it is viewed by others.

My sister and myself often strolled to the woods to gather nuts, or to hunt for the nests of birds— or stole away to a neighbouring stream to wade in the water. But we never went far from the house without having the fear of the Indians before our eyes. We had heard the story of our father's death so often repeated—had listened to so many similar legends—had so often witnessed the alarm created by a rumoured appearance of the Indians in the vicinity,—that our hearts had learned to quail in terror at the thought of a savage. The word *Indian* conveyed to our minds all that was fierce, and dangerous, and hateful. We knew what we had ourselves suffered from this ferocious race, and we saw that others lived in continual fear of them. We heard the men talk of " hunting Indians," as they would speak of tracking the beast of prey to his lair—and the women never met without speaking of the abduction of children, or the murder of females,—repeating tale after tale, each exceeding the former in horror, until the whole circle became agitated with fear, the candles seemed to burn blue, and the slightest sound was considered as a prognostic of instant massacre.

Many were our childish discussions and surmises on this all absorbing subject, as we played together.

"What made the Indians kill our father?" my little sister would ask, and we would guess and guess, without coming to any other conclusion than that it was "because they were bad people."

"Would they kill us?"—"Do they kill every body they meet?"—"Do they eat people?" were some of the questions which naturally occurred to us, and it will be readily believed that the agitation of them always led to inferences the most unfavourable to the Indian. If a bush rustled, or a footstep was heard as we strolled abroad, we imagined that the Indians were near; but, instead of running and screaming, as more civilised children would have done, we crept silently under the nearest cover, or dropped quietly in the high grass, with the instinct which teaches the young partridge a similar device—lying perfectly motionless, and throwing our little wild eyes vigilantly about until the danger had passed. We should not have moved had an Indian stepped over us; nor have betrayed any signs of life, so long as silence would have afforded concealment. Such are the habits of cunning and of self-command acquired, even in infancy, by those who live on a frontier exposed to hostile incursions—who are often in danger, and who hear continually of stratagems and deeds of violence.

Thus two years of my mother's widowhood had rolled away, when one day my sister and myself were amusing ourselves by dabbling in the water of a small branch not far from the house. She was at a distance from me—and, being intent on different objects, we had not spoken for some time—when suddenly I heard her utter a most piercing shriek. I looked up, and beheld her in the grasp of an Indian warrior. Instinctively I recoiled behind a thick bush, where I sat in breath-less silence, keeping my eye fixed on the savage, who, not having discovered me, began to retreat with his terrified prisoner in his arms. Poor child! I shall never forget the dreadful screams which she uttered—until the Indian, placing his hand on her mouth and menacing with his knife, gave her to understand that he would kill her unless she ceased to cry. Nor shall I ever fail to remember my own agony when I saw her borne away sobbing, stretching out her little arms, and gazing wildly towards her home for the last time. What rage and grief filled my young heart as I witnessed her pangs, and felt my own impotence —as the most beloved object in existence was torn from me, while I could neither prevent nor revenge the violence.

No sooner was the savage out of sight, than I started up and hurried to the house, taking care to follow the most concealed path, and treading

with the stealthy caution of the prowler of the
night. My uncle was not at home, and my poor
mother—my widowed, mourning mother, whose
infants were all that were left to her in this world
—words cannot describe the acuteness of the grief
with which she was overwhelmed. But she acted
with courage and prudence: displaying, in this
moment of affliction, a self-possession which never
forsook her under any circumstances. After my
father's death, I was perhaps the dearest object of
her affection. She felt at that moment the sentiment expressed by the patriarch of Israel: "If I
be bereaved of my children, I am bereaved."
Apprehending that the Indians still hovered around
the dwelling, and would soon appear to complete
their ferocious purpose, she closed the door and
placed the heaviest articles of furniture against it,
determined to defend herself to the last. She
said to me "Your father is dead, your sister is
gone, and you are all that is left to me—I must
save your life if I lose my own;" and then raising
one of the puncheons which formed the floor, she
thrust me under it, and charging me to lie still,
and neither move nor speak—whatever might
happen—restored the puncheon to its place. The
floor was sufficiently open to enable me to see
what passed, and sometimes to catch a glimpse of
the actors. It was now past sunset. In a few
minutes the Indians came to the door, and at-

tempted to force their way in ; but my mother
having a loaded rifle, presented it through a
crevice of the logs, upon which they retired,
uttering as they went the most horrible yells.
They soon returned, bearing lighted torches,
which they threw upon the roof—in a few minutes the house was in flames—the rifle dropped
from my mother's hands, and, before she could
determine what to do, the door was burst open,
and she was dragged out. The savages, finding
no other object upon which to vent their fury,
departed, carrying her with them.

I cannot pretend to convey any adequate idea
of my own emotions during this scene. The loss
of my little sister had gone to my heart—the
self-possession and energy of my mother had
awakened my admiration—and in the tumult of
other feelings, my own danger had scarcely been
the subject of a thought. I was naturally bold ;
and I was not given to the indulgence of selfish
reflections. But what a moment of horror was
it, when the house was fired, and the savages
rushed in ! When they laid their brutal hands
upon my mother, I experienced a sensation of
agony such as I had never known before. How
sacred is the person of a mother ! What pure
and hallowed affections cling around her ! What
sacrilege in the eyes of a sound hearted child, is
an act of violence against that parent, whose sex

claims the respect of her son, while her tenderness, her watchful solicitude, her devotion, her maternal pride, have entwined a thousand fond associations among the tendrils of his heart. Besides that intuitive love, which every mother kindles in the bosom of her offspring even before the will begins to exist, I had learned, young as I was, to reverence mine on account of her superior worth. Devoted to her children, I had witnessed more than one instance of her self-denial, which had penetrated my heart. I had seen her on several occasions display a degree of calmness in the presence of danger, and of patient fortitude under extreme suffering, which amounted, in my eyes, to heroism. I had beheld her widowed and in sorrow; and had begun to look forward to the time when I should be her protector. I had seen the involuntary tear trickling secretly down her cheek, and had listened, deeply affected, to the midnight prayer for her children, intended for the ear of Him only to whom it was addressed. A deed of violence perpetrated towards any other woman, would have struck me as brutal,—but there was a sacredness thrown around the person of my mother which gave to this proceeding a character of desecration. When I saw her forced away, I struggled to release myself from my confinement—I screamed—but the shouts of the infuriated incendiaries drowned my cries.

5

The flames were raging over my head, but I thought alone of my mother. The love of life was smothered by more powerful emotions, and I only wished to share her captivity, or to die in her arms.

The sounds of war died away. I no longer heard the footsteps of men, nor the yells of vengeance. The crackling of flames over my head, and the falling of firebrands upon the floor under which I was lying, alone met my ear. I was confused and stupefied by the ferocious deeds I had witnessed. A vague sense of my own danger began to stir within me. I looked round, and discovered that the space between the floor and the ground was sufficient to allow me room to crawl out. I crept from beneath the blazing pile, and found myself the sole spectator of that heart-rending scene of desolation. The perpetrators of that dark deed of aggression against the widow and the orphan, had fled with their captives. The flames were consuming the home which had sheltered me all the years of my existence of which I had any recollection—where I had played with my little sister, and had so often fallen asleep with my head upon my mother's bosom, and felt her warm kiss upon my lips, and had been awakend in the morning by her caresses. Here, morning and evening, had we knelt by her side, with our little hands pressed in hers, as she

prayed God to protect the bereaved and the helpless. A gush of tenderness overwhelmed my
heart, as the contemplation of my own desolate
wretchedness contrasted itself with past endearments. Around me was the darkness of the
night, rendered more black by the brightness of
the fire. I ran to my father's grave—for I could
not resist the conviction that the spirits of my
murdered mother and sister would hover over a
spot which was so sacred to us all. All was
silent here. The hand of the murderer, though
it may strike terror into the heart of the living,
cannot disturb the repose of the dead. I threw
myself on the ground. The reflection that I was
alone in the world became almost insupportable—
tears came to my relief—I wept bitterly.

In a little-while I recovered my composure. I
had been reared in habits which were not calculated to enervate my faculties; on the contrary, I
was thoughtful and daring. The idea occurred to
me that my mother and sister might still be
living, and could be rescued from captivity. No
sooner had this thought flashed upon my mind,
than I rushed, regardless of my own safety,
towards the house of our nearest neighbour. It
was two miles distant; but I was intimately acquainted with the path, and proceeded with a
speed which soon brought me to the place. Pale,
trembling, and in tears, I presented myself before

the astonished family, unable, at first, to articulate
any thing but the word " Indians!"

The effect produced by this alarming name, so
often heard, and so fraught with danger, was
instantaneous. All started up and prepared for
defence. The doors were closed, and the rifles
grasped. Consternation was painted on every
face ; but the men evinced a martial bearing, in
the alacrity with which they subdued their appre-
hensions, and flew to arms. When I told my
tale, however, in broken fragments, but intelligi-
bly enough for the comprehension of those who
were accustomed to such recitals, and it was
rendered probable that the savages were already
on their retreat, a different direction was given to
the feelings of this worthy family. Its head, a
strong, muscular man, slow, heavy, and apparently indolent, seemed to be inspired with a new
life.

" We must be after them, boys," said he, " they
haint got much start of us, no how—there'll be a
nice fresh trail in the morning that can't be
missed, and we can out travel the varmints, let
'em do their best."

" John !" exclaimed the wife, " you're a good
soul ! I wish I was a man, and could go along.
Can't you go to-night? Poor Sally Robinson—
she'll suffer a heap of misery before morning—the
distressed creetur !"

" Its no use to try to hunt Indians in the night,"
replied the man ; " and besides, it will take 'til
morning to get the neighbours warned in."

" Don't cry, Billy," said the woman, putting
her arms round my neck, and kissing me affectionately, " don't cry, my little man—they'll bring
your mammy back afore to-morrow night—no
mistake about that—its mighty hard for Indians
to get away from our people. You shall sleep
with my little boys, and be my son, 'til your
mammy comes back."

The backwoodsman now directed several young
men, his sons and others, who were present, to
mount their horses and spread the alarm through
the neighbourhood, and to summon all the men
to meet at his house the next morning. The
young fellows caught his ardour, and in a few
minutes were dashing off, through the woods, in
different directions.

There was little sleep among the inmates of
this cabin on that eventful night. The children
were afraid to go to bed. The man of the house,
whose name was Hickman, aware of the necessity
of husbanding all his powers for the approaching
chase, which might last several days, threw himself down in his clothes, and soon appeared to
slumber. His wife sat by the fire, sighing, pouring out bitter anathemas upon the Indians, and
giving utterance to her lively sympathy in the

5*

afflictions of her neighbour, while the children
crowded around her, squatted upon the floor with
their bare feet gathered under them, each clinging to some part of her dress, gazing at one
another in mute terror, or asking questions in
whispered and tremulous accents about the savages;—and all of them in turns casting glances
of pity at myself, as I sat, sometimes weeping
bitterly, and at other times staring in tearless
agony at the terrified group. At intervals, the
kind-hearted matron would articulate my mother's name, accompanied by passsionate expres-
sions of grief and affection.

"Poor Sally Robinson! she has had her own
troubles, poor thing! And she sich a good crec-
tur! It was sorrowful enough to be a lone woman,
—and her man murdered the way he was, right
before her eyes, as a body may say! The dear
knows how she did to stand it! Law, children,
don't pull my gownd so,—you'll tear every stitch
of clothes off of my back. What are you afeard
of? the Indians aint comin' here, no how,—the
varmints—they know better than for to go where
there's men about the house, 'drot their vile skins!
the 'bominable riff-raff cowardly scum of creation!
they haint got the hearts of men, no how! they
haint no more courage nor a burnt cracklin, no
way they can fix it! Poor Sally! ah me!—and
the dear child—the poor, poor little child!"

" Did the Indians kill little Sue, mammy ?"

" I don't know, child—they carried her off, and
Him that's above only knows what has become of
her. And they have burnt the very roof over the
heads of them that had no one to take care of
them."

" Did they burn Miss Robinson's house up,
mammy ?"

" To be sure they did—the cabin, and a beautiful piece of cloth that she had in the loom, and
all the plunder that the poor thing has been scrapin
together by the work of her own hands."

" Mammy,—"

" Hush, what's that ?"

Then they would all crowd together and listen.

" It's daddy snoring."

It was past midnight when the tramping of a
horse was heard rapidly approaching. The dogs
barked fiercely, as if conscious of the necessity of
unusual vigilance, and then ceased all at once. A
loud voice called, " Who keeps house ?"

Those who were sitting up were afraid to move ;
but Mr. Hickman, accustomed to awake at the
slightest alarm, started up, and proceeded, with
his gun in his hand, to open the door cautiously.
My uncle entered. He had heard the rumour
vaguely repeated, had hurried home, and found, in
the smoking embers of his dwelling, a fatal con-
firmation of his worst fears.

Between that time and the dawn of day the neighbours poured in, all armed, and prepared to pursue the Indians. Some were ready for action : others, who had repaired more hastily to the rendezvous, upon the moment of receiving the summons, now employed themselves in wiping out their guns, cleaning the locks, changing the flints, and supplying their pouches with all the munitions required for several days' service. Mr. Hickman seemed to be tacitly agreed upon as the leader. I watched all his motions, and, young as I was, saw with admiration the coolness and precision with which he made his arrangements. He examined every part of his rifle with the most severe scrutiny. He placed a handful of bullets on the table, and passed them rapidly through his fingers, one by one, to ascertain that they were perfectly round and smooth, rejecting those that were in the slightest degree defective. His flints and patches underwent the same close inspection. The tomahawk and knife were placed in his belt —then withdrawn and placed again—until the wary pioneer was satisfied that each was so arranged as to be capable of being quickly grasped by the hand, in case of sudden need, and so secured as not to be liable to be lost while the rider was dashing rapidly through the bushes. Grave and taciturn all the time, he was as cool as if preparing for a hunt.

His wife hung round him during these operations,—now officiously tendering her services—now leaning on his shoulder, and speaking to him in a low voice,—then retiring, as if overcome by her fears, and sometimes secretly wiping away a tear with the corner of her apron.

"John," she would say, "you won't lose no time, I hope. Poor Sally! she will be mighty bad off 'till she sees you comin—it's sich a dreadful bad fix for any body to be in."

"We sha'nt be long, I reckon."

"Take mighty good care of yourself, John—you know, dear, what a poor broken-hearted body I'd be without you. Don't ride Ball,—you know he stumbles powerful bad, and falls down sometimes—and his sight's so bad, he aint no account, no how, in the night."

"I shall ride Dick—no mistake in him."

"No two ways about Dick," reiterated the wife; "boys, go and feed Dick, and clean him, and fix him good for your daddy to ride. And, John, when you get up to the miserable varmints, don't be too ambitious—you know you're apt to be sort o' quick when you're raised—don't be too brash; if you can only get poor Sally Robinson away from them, don't run no risks. You don't reckon you'll have to fight with them, do you?"

"It's a little mixed," replied the husband.

"It would be a droll way to hunt Indians, and

not kill any of them," interrupted one of the party.

"I'll be dogged if I don't save one of them," added another.

"I allow to use up one or two," continued a third.

"I'll never agree to return 'til we use up the whole gang—stock, lock, and barrel," added another.

"They are the darndest puteranimous villyens on the face of the whole yearth—and 1 go in for puttin the pewter to 'em, accordin' to law," chimed in a little dried up old man, who was whetting his knife against the side of the fire-place, and looking as savage as a meat-axe. It was very obvious that the Indians would get no quarter.

At daylight the party began to mount. All were completely equipped. Under every saddle was a blanket, to save the horse's back—behind it was tied either a great coat or a blanket to sleep in—on this was lashed a wallet, containing several days' provisions, and a tin cup dangled on the top of the whole. Each man carried a good rifle, in complete order, and had a knife and a tomahawk in his belt. Their legs were covered, to protect them from the briars, with dressed deer-skin—not made into any garment, but rolled tightly round the limb and tied with strings. Some wore shoes, others moccasins—some had hats, others rejected this covering, and wore only a cotton handkerchief bound closely round the head. When mounted they bade adieu to their friends, and set out in high spirits—not observing any particular order of march at first, but falling gradually into the single file, as the most convenient arrangement for passing rapidly through the forest.

Towards evening two of the party returned. They brought the clothes of my sister which had been found by the way, near the bank of the Ohio, torn and bloody, but yet in a state to be identified. There was other evidence, abundant and conclusive, that the poor child had been murdered, and her body thrown into the river. I cannot express the poignancy of my sensations on receiving the intelligence of this catastrophe. I had, until now, sustained my spirits by the hope of her escape. I would not believe that even a savage could wantonly give pain, much less inflict death, upon my innocent companion—a sweet, rosy, laughing girl. A girl! a *little* girl—I could not imagine it possible that any human creature, with the form of manhood, would touch the life of a thing so winning, so gentle, so helpless. I dreamed away the day in painful excitement—in feverish visions of hope and fear; but when the truth came I sunk down in an agony of grief and horror. I had not realised the possibility of a catastrophe so terrible.

Another day was drawing near to a close. I

was withering under the pressure of affliction.
Grief, watching, excitement, and loss of appetite,
had produced a bodily exhaustion, attended with
extreme nervous sensibility. I had wandered off
by myself, and came, I hardly know how, to the
blackened ruins of our cabin. I seated myself
under a tree, in the desolated yard. It was a
bright calm evening ; the sun was sinking towards
the horizon, and the long shadows of the forest
extended over the spot. The cool air fanned my
burning brow, and brought a momentary sense of
relief from pain. Before me was a silent heap of
ashes—but all else wore the air of home. A few
fruit trees that stood scattered around, were in
full blossom, and the bees were humming busily
among the flowers—the birds sang, and the domestic animals seemed to welcome my return.
The cow, that had been standing unmilked, came
lowing towards me—the pigs ran to meet me—
and the fowls gathered about the place where I
sat, as if they recognised a master whose protection had been withdrawn from them. Oh ! how
many ties there are to bind the soul to earth !
When the strongest are cut asunder, and the
spirit feels itself cast loose from every bond which
connects it with mortality, how imperceptibly
does one little tendril after another become entwined about it, and draw it back with gentle
violence ! He who thinks he has but one love is

always mistaken. The heart may have one overmastering affection, more powerful than all the rest, which, like the main root of the tree, is that which supports it ; but if that be cut away, it will find a thousand minute fibres still clinging to the soil of humanity. An absorbing passion may fill up the soul, and while it lasts, may throw a shade over the various obligations, and the infinite multitudes of little kindnesses, and tender associations, that bind us to mankind ; but when that fades, these are seen to twinkle in the firmament of life, as the stars shine, after the sun has gone down. Even the brute, and the lilies of the field, that neither toil nor spin, put in their silent claims; and the heart that would have spurned the world, settles quietly down again upon its bosom. A moment before, I was in despair ;—and now I was caressing the dumb animals around me. They seemed like friends; and a something like joy revived within me, as I reflected that I was not entirely forsaken. I raised my eyes and my heart to Heaven, with a feeling of thanksgiving, and melted into tenderness.

I looked up and gazed around me. In the edge of the forest, an object attracted my attention. It was the dim and shadowy representation of a human figure. It moved; and then seemed to lean against a tree; again it moved, and halted. Could it be an Indian? Was the savage thirst

6

for blood not yet sated? Were they not to be
satisfied until all, even the last, of my unhappy
family, should have fallen under the tomahawk?
I did not fly: I would not have moved from that
spot had a myriad of savages appeared,—a legion
of devils could not have daunted my spirit in that
moment of stubborn desperation. The figure
moved along under the shade of a long point of
timber, which approached to within a few yards
of the house—advancing, and then halting, cautiously as an insidious enemy, or painfully like a
friend, who came the bearer of unwelcome tidings.
I watched it with intense interest, until it came
near, and stepped from under the woody covert,
which had rendered the form indistinct,—and
then I recognised, with unerring instinct, the
person of my mother. I rushed towards her, and
in a moment was in her arms. I gazed at her
with an overwhelming gush of joy and fondness—
but, oh! how changed, how wretched was she!
Her bare feet were torn and bloody—her clothes
were tattered into shreds—her eyes red—her
face pale and emaciated—her frame exhausted
with fatigue. After being driven forward a whole
day, she had effected her escape in the night, and
had wandered back to the home which had been
desolated by the ruthless hand of the murderer and
incendiary. With my assistance she was enabled,
with much difficulty, to crawl to the house of our

kind neighbour, where she sunk down under her
bodily and mental sufferings, and remained some
days dangerously ill.

The party who had gone to her assistance, had
missed her on the way, but had overtaken the
Indians, and attacked them with such spirit, that
one half the savages were slain in the first onset.
The remainder dispersed, and found safety in
flight.

We did not return to the spot which had proved
so calamitous to our unhappy family, but removed
to a place which was supposed to be less exposed
to danger. I had now no companion. The loss
of my little sister preyed upon my spirits. She
was continually the subject of my thoughts. I
often sat for hours together absorbed in visionary
speculations, founded upon the possibility of my
sister's escape from death. As is the case with
all dreamers, I did not examine the evidence for
the purpose of learning the truth, nor did I permit
the certainty of the catastrophe which had befallen her to interfere with my theories; but
assuming the premises which were necessary, I
proceeded to erect an airy superstructure, and to
luxuriate in the enjoyment of the "baseless fabric
of a vision." I exercised my ingenuity in imagining a variety of modes in which she might have
escaped from her captors, fancied for her some
present state of existence under the protection of

kind benefactors, and realised the joy of her sudden and unexpected restoration. Sometimes I supposed her to be living in captivity, and fancied myself leading an armed party to her rescue— I went through all the stratagems and perils of border warfare—signalised myself by a series of acts of almost miraculous daring—delivered my beloved sister from bondage, and filled the heart of my bereaved mother with joy and pride. When I slept, the same fancies were ever present. I strolled about with my sister, embarrassed by the endeavour to reconcile the appearances of my dream with the facts indelibly engraved upon my memory. Sometimes she sat by me, with her hand clasped in mine, and narrated a series of adventures, which she had passed through since our parting; but more frequently she seemed to laugh at my credulity, and pronounced our misfortunes to have been all a dream. Often did I awake in tears.

As I grew older, my tenderness began to give way to sterner feelings. Accustomed to fear the Indians from infancy, I began at last to hate them with intense malignity. I had never heard them spoken of but as enemies, to extirpate whom was a duty. I had been taught to consider the slaying of an Indian as an act of praiseworthy public spirit. As my sorrow for the sufferings of those who were dear to me began to harden into indig-

nation, the desire of revenge was kindled in my
bosom. This feeling was rapidly developed, because it was the only one connected with my
reveries which I could trace out to any practical
result. I could not bring my sister to life, nor
dispel the cloud of grief from the face of my
widowed mother : but I could strike the savage, I
could burn his dwelling, and desolate his fireside,
as he had desolated mine. This passion soon
gained a predominating mastery over my mind—
as a rank weed shoots up and overshadows those
around it, the desire of revenge struck deep its
roots, grew rapidly into vigour, and smothered
the better emotions of my heart.

I procured a gun, and began to roam the forest.
In this country boys are permitted, at an early
age, to mingle in the sports of men, and my propensity for hunting did not excite any particular
remark. The hunters sometimes took me with
them ; but more often I wandered about alone. I
soon learned to shoot with precision, and became
expert in many of the devices of the backwoodsman.

When I was about twelve years old, a village
was laid out in the neighbourhood in which we
then resided. The country was settling rapidly ;
several wealthy families from Virginia were
among the emigrants ; the frontier had been

6*

further west, and with it had rolled the tide of
war. Society began to be organised, and many
of the luxuries of social life were introduced.
Among other improvements was a school, conducted by a person of some erudition, who brought
with him a good many books, and was looked
upon as a prodigy of knowledge.

I was sent to school; entered upon my studies
with eagerness, and made rapid advances in learning. With a mind naturally inquisitive, and accustomed to rely upon itself, I had no difficulty in
mastering any task which was given me, and soon
became fond of reading. My teacher had in his
possession a number of volumes of history, which
I perused with avidity. A few classics, which
fell into my hands, I read over and over, with the
delight of a newly awakened admiration. I commenced the study of the Latin language, and
gained a slight acquaintance with the mythology
and history of the ancients. In three years, my
character was much changed; my mind was enlarged, my affections softened, and the tone of my
morals considerably ameliorated. I still loved my
gun, and indulged my propensity for wandering in
the forest; while my hatred of the Indians, and
that thirst for vengeance over which I had so long
brooded, were by no means blunted by the perusal
of those histories, in which the recitals of military
daring form a prominent part, and martial accom-

plishments are held up as exemplary virtues worthy of the highest admiration.

I was little more than fifteen years of age, when a number of the poorer families in the neighbourhood formed a party for the purpose of removing to the settlements upon the Mississippi, in Illinois —a new country, which just then began to be spoken of. My uncle and mother determined to accompany them. I know not what infatuation induced them to brave again the perils of the wilderness, after all their fatal experience. It is probable that their only inducement was that love of new lands, of fresh wild scenery, and of the unconstrained habits of border life, which forms a ruling passion with the people of the backwoods, and which no chastening from the hand of adversity can eradicate.

The only settlements of the Americans in Illinois, at that time, were in the neighbourhood of the French villages, which were scattered along the American Bottom, on the Mississippi, from Kaskaskia to the vicinity of St. Louis. We embarked in two large boats; and, after floating quietly down the Ohio to the Mississippi, began to ascend that wonderful river, proceeding slowly against its powerful current. Sometimes a fair wind invited us to hoist our sails, and enabled us for a while to move forward without labour; but usually our boats were pushed with poles, by the

most severe manual exertion. To get forward at
all in opposition to the current, it was necessary
to creep along close to the shore. But there
were places where it became impossible to make
any headway even by this method: where the
bank was perpendicular, the water too deep to
allow the use of poles, and the headlong stream
swept foaming against the shore. In such emer-
gencies it was impossible to proceed, except by
means of the *cordelle*, a strong cable attached to
the boat, by which the boatmen, walking on the
shore, dragged it past these dangerous places.
The shores, on both sides, were inhabited by
Indians, and our labours were rendered the more
burthensome, by the necessity of keeping up a
continual watch to prevent surprise.

One day we reached a place where the river is
closely hemmed in by rock on either side, and the
stream, confined within a more narrow space than
it usually occupies, rushes with great impetuosity
through the strait. It is one of the most difficult
passes on the river for ascending boats. Here, of
course, neither oars nor poles could be of any
avail, and arrangements were made for using the
cordelle. My uncle and mother were in the foremost boat—I had happened to be, for the moment,
in the other, which, by some accident, was detained, so as to fall a short distance into the rear.
The leading boat passed round a little point of

land, which concealed it from our view, and immediately afterwards we heard the reports of several rifles. The Indians had formed an ambuscade at the point where they knew the crew must land to use the cable, and had fallen upon them at a moment when the difficulties of the navigation absorbed their attention so entirely, that they had forgotten their usual precautions, and were not prepared either to fight or fly. On hearing the alarm we endeavoured to hasten to their assistance, aided by a breeze which filled our sail, and bore us rapidly along. But we were too late; and, on turning the point, beheld the other boat moored fast to the shore, and in possession of a hellish band of savage warriors, who were dashing furiously about on the deck and on the bank, uttering the most hideous yells. We came near enough to see the bodies of our friends stretched lifeless on the ground, or struggling in the agonies of death—surrounded by the monsters, who were still beating them with clubs, and gratifying their demoniac thirst for blood in gashing with their knives the already mutilated corpses. Never did I behold a scene of such horror: language has no power to describe it, nor the mind capacity to obliterate its impressions. Men, women, and children, were alike the victims of an indiscriminating carnage. The hell-hounds were literally tearing them in pieces,—exulting, shouting, smearing themselves with blood, and trampling on the remains of their wretched victims.

On our approach, they prepared for a new triumph; for their numbers so greatly exceeded our own as to render victory certain. We had advanced so near as to be within the range of a heavy fire which they poured in, and the foaming current seemed to be dashing us upon the rocks on which they stood—when our steersman, a cool experienced man, suddenly threw the head of the boat across the river, in the opposite direction, and causing the sail to be trimmed suitably, shot rapidly away from the scene of the massacre. A shout of rage and disappointment burst from our crew, who were thoughtlessly preparing to revenge their friends. It was well that a more prudent head directed our motions. The dead were beyond the reach of our aid, and the infuriated savages, mad with victory, greatly outnumbered ourselves. We found safety on the opposite shore, where we remained in painful suspense until the murderers retired, when we repaired to the melancholy spot, and rendered, in silent agony, the last sad rites to the remains of the fallen. Not one of all that crew had escaped. I recognised, with difficulty, the mangled bodies of my mother and my uncle; and kneeling beside the remains of my parent, swore eternal vengeance against her murderers—against that race who had poisoned the cup of her existence,—and, not content with robbing her of all that made life dear, and of life itself, had insulted her inanimate remains.

Enough of this. I cannot express the feelings of a son under such circumstances—the only son of a widowed mother—who had been almost her sole companion, had shared her adversity, witnessed her afflictions, and appreciated her maternal fondness. I pass them over.

I began to lead a new life. I found myself at Kaskaskia, a stranger. I had not a relative living, and in this place I had no acquaintances. But my story gained me much sympathy; I was kindly received—every door was open to me, and every heart seemed to feel that I had claims upon my countrymen.

No degree of kindness, however, could soothe my excited feelings. The determination to avenge my mother's death,—to be revenged for the loss of a father, a sister, and an uncle, was unalterably formed, and thirst for the blood of the savage was become an uncontrollable passion. I wandered about in the woods and over the prairies—spending my whole time in hunting, in increasing my skill in the use of the rifle, and in rendering more perfect my proficiency in the various devices of the hunter. In my wanderings I became acquainted with a Frenchman, who lived almost entirely in the forest. He was a small, slender,

quiet man, past the meridian of life. Taciturn
and inoffensive, he subsisted by hunting and fishing, and had little communion with his own species.
He was never engaged in war, or in any kind of
altercation. Equally friendly with the whites and
the Indians, he visited the villages and the camps
of both, and was well received, although occasionally suspected by each of acting as a spy for the
other. This suspicion was founded on the singu-
larity of his character, in which a great degree of
ignorance and childish simplicity was combined
with a remarkable shrewdness in matters connected with his own vocation. The latter was
very naturally supposed to arise from native sagacity, and the former to be the result of profound
dissimulation. What the truth might be, I never
knew; but, to me, Peter seemed to ·be the most
unsophisticated of human beings. How it happened that I gained his confidence, does not now
occur to me; for he was unsocial in his habits—
and although, when he visited the French villages,
he cheerfully partook of the hospitality of his
countrymen, conversed freely, and was a delighted
spectator of their festivities, he soon wandered off,
and was not seen again for weeks, or even months.

To this singular being I attached myself, and
became the companion of his voluntary banishment
from society. We retired far from the settlements, avoiding equally the hunting grounds of

the Indians and the haunts of the white people. Sometimes we encamped at a secluded spot on the margin of a river, and spent our time in fishing. Then we wandered away to the pastures of the deer, living upon venison, and drying the skins of our game. Again, we sought the retreats of the beaver, and, setting our traps, reposed quietly in the neighbouring coverts to witness the success of our arts. Occasionally we crept upon the elk or the buffalo, and engaged, with the hunter's ardour, in the pursuit of these noble animals; and sometimes we circumvented the cunning of the wild cat, or planned the destruction of the wolf or the panther. To add variety to our meals, we plundered the hoard of the wild bee; and Peter soon taught me to trace the industrious insect through the air, from the flowery prairie, to his distant home in the forest. When our supply of furs became considerable, we collected them from their different places of deposit at some point on the river, and, embarking in a canoe, floated down to the nearest village, where we exchanged them for powder, lead, and other necessaries.

But I did not spend all my time in hunting and fishing. Naturally observant, the little education I had received had quickened my mental powers, and rendered me keenly inquisitive into all the arcana of nature. I noticed every thing around me;—the appearances of the clouds, and the

7

changes of the weather—the foliage of the trees,
and the growth of the multitudinous vegetation of
the wilderness—the habits of animals, and the
various notes of the inhabitants of the forest,—
but especially all the appearances of nature—all
the varieties of sunlight and shade—all the diver-
sities in the aspect of the natural scenery, from
midnight to noon, attracted my attention. Peter,
although not a naturalist, was an admirable teacher
in these studies. Accustomed to observe nature
from his infancy, he had become acquainted with
the secrets of the great volume, which all profess
to admire and but few understand. He could anticipate the changes of the weather. He knew
when the moon would rise, and when the deer
would be stirring. He could select, with ready
tact, the most suitable pool for fishing, and could
tell the hour at which the fish would bite. His
ear was acute in distinguishing sounds: if a wolf
stole past in the dark, he could detect the fall of
his stealthy footstep in the rustling of the leaf or
the cracking of the twigs; and when the owl
hooted at midnight, he knew whether that scream
denoted the presence of an intruder, or was the
ordinary note with which the solitary bird solaced
his hour of recreation. There were few appearances, and few sounds, which Peter could not
explain. He knew the points of the compass
and the landmarks of the country, and could find

his way in the dark as well as in the daylight,
and under a clouded atmosphere as easily as in
the blaze of noon.

Under such tuition, I soon became also an expert woodsman. With an enterprising mind, a
frame naturally vigorous, and habits formed from
infancy upon the frontier, I had little to learn. I
only needed experience, and this I now gained in
the school of practice. The backwoodsman acquires great skill in the use of the rifle, because he
employs that weapon not merely in sport, but in the
pursuit of a serious occupation. It was particularly
so in those early times. If he made war, it was
usually at his own cost; if he hunted, it was to procure a livelihood. In his long marches through the
woods, when he is absent several days, or perhaps
weeks, from home, he can carry but little ammunition, and has no means of renewing his supply
when it becomes expended. Powder and lead are
scarce and costly in these secluded neighbourhoods. He is therefore cautious not to throw
away a charge, and seldom fires at random. He
creeps upon his enemy, or his game, gains every
available advantage, measures his distance, and
takes his aim, with great deliberation and accu-
racy. In any attainment, it is not practice
merely which secures perfection, but it is the
habit of careful practice, of always doing well that
which is to be done, and of aiming continually at

improvement. Such is the habit of our hunters, who seldom discharge their rifles unnecessarily, and who feel their own characters, and that of their guns, at stake in every shot which they fire.

There was one subject, however, which occupied my mind especially—one master purpose, to which every feeling of my heart, and every employment of my life, was subservient. My thirst for revenge was unbounded. It filled up my whole soul. I thought of little else than schemes for the destruction of the savage. I was maturing a stupendous plan of vengeance, and bringing all the resources of my mind to bear upon this one subject. The feet of men are swift to shed blood. I improved rapidly in the arts of destruction. I practised all the deceptive stratagems, by which the hunter conceals himself from an enemy, or baffles the instinct of the brute. I could lie for hours so still, that a person, within a few feet of me, would not have suspected that a living creature was near him ; and concealed myself so successfully, that even the Indian would not have discovered me, unless he stepped by accident on my body. I could swim, and dive, and lie all day in the water, with my head hidden among the rushes, watching for prey. I learned especially that patience, that forbearance, that entire mastery over my appetites, fears, and passions, which enables the Indian to submit to any

privation, and to delay the impending blow until
all his plans are ripe, however alluring may be
the temptation for premature action.

I concealed my design from all, even from my
companion, Peter, while I was every day getting
from him the information requisite to advance
my purpose. I ascertained the names of the surrounding tribes, their dispositions in respect to
the whites, and the location of their villages. I
obtained the names of their most celebrated
warriors, and particularly of such as were distinguished by deeds of violence against my countrymen. But the information to which I listened
with the most thrilling interest, and treasured in
my inmost heart, related to the massacre of my
mother. I learned from the Frenchmen, that the
party which perpetrated that bloody deed, consisted of a number of desperate individuals from
different villages, led by a lawless chief, who still
occasionally assembled the band for similar out-
rages. I treasured with pertinacious care the
names of those Indians, and the distinctive marks
by which they might be known. More than once,
when I heard that they were hunting in our neighbourhood, I left my companion, silently tracked
their footsteps day after day, laid concealed by
the path along which they passed, or crept
secretly upon their camp; until by close observation I made myself acquainted with their persons.

7*

All this was the more difficult, because this band,
aware of the indignation which that unprovoked
murder had excited, avoided the white people, and
were constantly on their guard against surprise.
But what vigilance can guard against the watchful cunning of revenge—revenge for the cold-
blooded butchery of a mother, a sister, and a
father, and the disruption of every tie which binds
a young and generous heart to existence !

At length the long sought opportunity presented
itself. In the fall of the year succeeding that of
the massacre, I discovered that the hated band
were hunting on the margin of the Mississippi,
and were in the custom of retiring for safety,
every night, to an island in that river—first
making their fire, and arranging their camp on
the shore of the main land, as if with the intention of spending the night there, and then secretly
stealing away to the island under the cover of
darkness.

I went to the nearest settlement—where my
story was well known, and had awakened a generous sympathy—and laying aside my usual reserve,
boldly announced my plan, and asked for a band
of volunteers to assist in its execution. Such a
call was, at that period, seldom made in vain.
Warlike in their habits, and inveterately hostile
to the savages, the people of the frontier were
always ready for excursions of this character.

On this occasion the excitement was the more easily kindled, because others had been bereaved of relatives and friends, in the same catastrophe which deprived me of my last parent, and all were indignant at that outrage. The plan was well matured, and rapidly executed. A company was raised, equal in number to the Indians, all picked men, and completely equipped. At midnight, we assembled secretly on the bank of the river, far above the island, and embarking in canoes, floated quietly down. The night was cloudy, and so perfectly dark, as to render it impossible that we should be discovered from either shore. The stream bore us along, and the noiseless paddle accelerated and directed the motion of the canoe, without creating the slightest sound which could awaken alarm. We landed on the island without confusion, and pursued the meanders of the shore until we found the canoes of the enemy. These we cut adrift, and pursuing a dim path, came to the camp where the savages were lying asleep, around the embers of a fire,—all but a sentinel, who, half awake, sat upon a log. Each man selected his object, in accordance with a preconcerted plan—took a deliberate aim, and fired ;— and then drawing our tomahawks, we rushed in, and grappled the astonished savages as they sprung to their feet. So complete was the surprise, that they had not time to grasp their arms before the tomahawk was busy among them. A few seized the nearest weapon, and fought with desperation. But the conflict was soon over :—not one of that fated band escaped to tell of their defeat. Morning dawned over a scene reposing in beautiful and majestic quiet; its rosy light streaming over the variegated foliage, and glancing from the eddies and ripples of the turbid river —and there we sat, a grim and bloody company, brooding over the gashed and mutilated bodies of the slain, while a few scouts were busily exploring the island, to ascertain whether any of the enemy were yet lurking in the bushes. Not one was found , and we departed in triumph,—in that silent and subdued triumph which the sight of the slain inspires in the bosom of the generous victor, but yet with the emotions of satisfaction which men feel, who believe that they have performed a duty.

I had supposed, previous to this event, that the gratification of my revenge would give peace to my bosom ; but this is a passion which grows stronger by indulgence ; and no sooner had I tasted the sweets of vengeance, than I began to feel an insatiable thirst for the blood of the savage. Resuming my secluded habits, but without rejoining my former companion, I now lived entirely in the woods, occupied with my own thoughts, and pursuing, systematically, a plan of warfare against

that hated race whom I regarded with invincible
animosity. I followed the footsteps of their hunting parties, eagerly watching for an opportunity
to cut off any straggler who might wander away
from the others. For whole days I would lie concealed by the paths which they travelled, or near
a spring which they frequented; and if a single
Indian presented himself, I shot him down without
remorse, as I would have slain a wolf, or crushed
a rattlesnake. Sometimes I met a single warrior
openly, and we fought manfully, hand to hand:
that I was successful in those conflicts, is proved
by the fact that I am alive—for those single com-
bats are usually fatal to one of the parties. But
more frequently I sought to engage them under
every advantage which might ensure success, not
feeling the obligation of any point of honour
which obliged me to meet an Indian on fair terms.
It happened, of course, that the advantage was
sometimes on their side; occasionally, I fell in,
accidentally, with several of their warriors, or was
tracked and pursued by a party—and then I
eluded them by cunning, or escaped by superior
swiftness of foot. They soon learned to know me
as their enemy, and scoured the woods in search
of me, with an eagerness equal to my own; but
while they sought my life by every artifice known
to savage warfare, few of them were willing to
meet me single-handed; for it is well understood,

that where the white man is trained to this species
of hostility, he is superior to the Indian, because
his physical powers are greater, and his courage
of a higher and more generous tone.

At length, tired of the monotony of the life I
led, and sated with carnage, I retired from the
woods, and betook myself to farming, living a
quiet and industrious life, and only resuming my
former habits to join a hunting party, or to assist
with others in the defence of the frontiers, in case
of an alarm.   Once in a great while, however,
after a longer interval of quiet than usual, I took
my rifle, and strolled off to the woods to kill an
Indian, as another man would seek recreation in
hunting a deer or a panther.

It seems unnatural that a man should pursue a life that may appear so ferocious and even
unprincipled.   But you must not forget that I had
been raised upon the frontier ; that I had been
accustomed from infancy to hear the Indian
spoken of as an enemy—as a cowardly, malevo-
lent, and cruel savage, who stole upon the unprotected, in the hour of repose, and murdered without respect to age or sex ; that many atrocities
had been perpetrated within my own knowledge,
or related to me by those who had seen them ;
and that I had suffered more than others by this
detested race.   Those who know the relations of
mutual aggression, and continual alarm, which

existed between the pioneers and the Indians, in the first settlement of the country, can easily imagine that the hatred they felt towards each other was intense and permanent; and that an individual, who considered himself more deeply injured than the rest, might naturally have supposed himself justifiable in seeking a more than ordinary measure of retaliation.

I come now to a circumstance which changed the tone of my feelings, and the whole colour of my life. One day, towards the close of summer, I had gone out bee-hunting. Our practice was to find the bee-trees, at our leisure, during the summer, and mark them with a tomahawk; each hunter used his own mark, and respected those of others; and at the proper season, we went out with some axe-men, and proper vessels, cut down the trees, and collected the honey. I had set out early, and spent the day in roaming over a wild unfrequented tract, in search of trees. To find them, I watched the bees, observing, as they left the flowers, clogged with honey, the course they flew—or I set bee-bait, usually a little salt and water, in an open vessel, which these insects sip greedily, and then marked the direction of their flight. The bee, in returning home, always flies in a direct line; and the experienced hunter, having observed the course, can follow it so accurately, that he seldom fails to find the tree. This

he is enabled to do, partly by knowing the
kind of trees to examine, and partly by the
acuteness of his eye and ear, which enables him,
when near the place, to see the insects hover-
ing about it, or to hear the hum of those busy
labourers.

I delighted in this employment. I loved to sit
in the edge of the prairie, and gaze upon its undulating surface, to see the waving of the tall
grass as the wind swept over it, to mark the
various colours of the flowers, to follow the laborious bee in her active flight along the plain, to
behold the celerity and skill with which she
gathered her harvest of sweets from this immense
garden, and to trace her through the air as she
darted away, laden with spoil, to her forest home.
I loved the quiet of this solitary sport. The
admirer of nature always reaps instruction in gazing upon her scenes of native luxuriance. The
wisdom of Providence is so infinite, the ingenuity
displayed in all the arcana of the animal and
vegetable creation is so diversified, that every day
thus spent discloses new facts, and suggests a
novel train of reflection. In the few years I had
spent at school, I had read enough to excite
curiosity, and to invigorate the powers of thought;
and so indelibly were those studies impressed upon
my memory, that the classic images of the
ancient writers arose continually in my mind, and

furnished pleasing illustrations of those natural appearances by which I was surrounded.

On that day, my mind, thus calmed by an agreeable train of association, had wandered back to the period of childhood, and I thought of the sister who had been my companion, and whose death I had so amply revenged. I tried to recall her features, and the sports in which we had engaged together. I speculated on what she might have become, had the ruthless hand of the savage spared her to grow up to maturity. She would now have attained the bloom of womanhood, and her softness would have restrained those fierce passions, the long indulgence of which had hardened my heart, and thrown a gloom over my mind. She would perhaps have been a wife and a mother; my affections would have become entwined with those of other beings, and, instead of being a solitary man, standing alone in the world, like the blasted and wind-shaken tree of the prairie, I should have grown up surrounded by hearts allied to my own, and have struck down my roots into the soil, and interlocked my branches with those of my kindred.

I had begun, very recently, to doubt the propriety of cherishing those feelings of implacable resentment, which I had indulged through my whole life, of brooding over the melancholy disasters of my youth, and of pursuing that systematic

8

plan of destruction, which kept my hand continually imbued in blood, and my mind agitated
by the tempest of passion. Not that I questioned
for a moment my right to destroy the savage:—
that was a principle too deeply ingrained in my
nature to be eradicated—the dreadful maxim of
revenge was pricked upon my heart with the point
of a sharp instrument, and the characters stood
there indelibly recorded. Filial piety sanctioned
the promptings of nature ; and I believed that in
killing a savage I performed my duty as a man,
and served my country as a citizen. But I had
begun to discover the injurious effects of my mode
of life upon my own character and happiness. It
had rendered me moody and unsocial. It kept
me estranged from society, encouraged a habit of
self-torture, and perpetuated a chain of indignant
and sorrowful reflections. I saw that others forgave injury, and forgot bereavement ; the cloud
passed over them, like the storm of the summer
day, black and terrible in its fury, but brief in its
continuance, and the sunshine of peace beamed
out again upon them—while I had disdained consolation, had fled the kindness of fellow-creatures,
and had repelled the healing balm which Providence pours into the wounds of the afflicted.

Occupied by such thoughts, the day wore away,
the sun was sinking in the west, and I entered a
thick wood, for the purpose of making my camp

for the night, on the margin of a small river that
meandered through it. Habitually cautious, I approached the place with noiseless steps, when I
perceived, on the bank of the stream, the hunting-
lodge of an Indian—a slight shelter, made by
throwing a few mats over some poles which were
stuck in the ground. I examined the priming of
my rifle, loosened my knife in its sheath, changed
a little my direction, so as to advance against the
wind, and crept stealthily upon the unguarded
hunter. He was stretched on the ground, lazily
sleeping away the afternoon, and was not armed
nor painted—having evidently sought this quiet
spot, with his family, for the purpose of supporting
them by fishing. His wife, whose back was towards me, was busily engaged in some domestic
employment; a child, perfectly naked, was wal-
lowing in the sand, and another, an infant, was
lashed to a board which leaned against a tree near
the mother. All were silent. I crept up with
the noiseless motion of a disembodied spirit, intending to despatch the hunter as he lay inert
upon the ground. I had never yet spared a
warrior of that race; and, as my contempt for
them prevented me from feeling any pride in such
exploits, I exulted in the prospect of an easy
victory. All the reasoning of that day faded at
once from my mind; but the recollections of my
childhood, which had been called up, gave a fresh-

ness to my desire for revenge. I had never aimed
a blow against a woman or a child; they were
sacred from any violence at my hand. But when
I saw that Indian father, with his wife and his two
children, the coincidence in the number and ages
of the family reminded me of the fireside of my
father, as it must have been when desolated by his
death; and I felt a malignant delight in the idea
of invading this family as mine had been invaded,
and blasting their peace by crushing their protector, *there*, on that very spot, in the presence of his
innocent and helpless dependents. He was completely in my power: I could shoot him from the
spot where I stood. There was no chance for his
escape. But I approached still nearer. We were
separated but a few paces, and I stood behind the
trunk of a large tree, which completely concealed
me. Once he expanded his nostrils, as if the scent
of a white man had reached him—and once he
turned his ear towards the ground, as if the sound
of a footstep vibrated upon it; but his indolence
prevailed over his vigilance.

I was about to raise my rifle, for the purpose of
firing, when the woman turned her face towards
me and stood erect. I had before remarked that
her stature was taller than that of the squaws, who
are usually short, and that her hair, which hung
plaited in one thick roll down her back, was not
black,—and I now saw that she was not of Indian

descent. Although browned by long exposure to the weather, her features and complexion were those of my own countrywomen. But what struck me most, and almost deprived me of my self-possession, was her likeness to my deceased mother. Had it not been for the difference of age, I should have been persuaded that my parent stood before me. The height, the figure, the complexion, the expression of countenance, were all so similar, that, notwithstanding the Indian costume in which the female before me was clad, she was the exact representation of my mother, as I recollected her in my early years—not as I remembered her in after times, when broken down by widowhood and suffering.

A thought rushed across my mind. The age of that young woman corresponded with the years to which my sister would have attained, had she lived. What a gush of feeling overwhelmed and almost burst my heart, as this suspicion arose—what delight, what indignation! Could it be possible that my sister had survived, and that I found her thus—the wife of a savage, the mother of a spurious offspring of that degraded race! My arm sunk, the gun rested on the ground, and I leaned against the tree. I stood for a long while watching the group with intense interest—pursuing the female especially with an eye of eager curiosity. In what slight circumstances do we

8*

discover resemblance! When she moved, there
was the air of my mother; if she spoke to her
children, there was the voice; if she smiled, there
was my mother's smile. My parent had been
handsomer than most women, and this young female,—though her features were hardened by toil
and weather, though the wildness of the Indian
glance was in her eye, and the vacancy of ignorance was in her countenance,—was yet beautiful,
and like my mother!

Convinced that I saw my sister, conflicting
emotions took possession of my mind, and I became irresolute of purpose. At one moment I
felt more determined than ever to slay the Indian,
whose alliance with my only relative I considered
a new insult, and a deeper injury than all others;
then I melted into tenderness as I gazed on her.
I looked at her children, and recoiled at the idea
of the unnatural union which had brought them
into existence—I looked at herself, and felt the
stirrings of a brother's affection.

At last I determined to resolve my doubts; and,
subduing every appearance of emotion, I emerged
from my concealment and walked slowly towards
the lodge. On discovering me, the woman, without betraying her surprise, uttered a low admo-
nition to her husband, who arose to receive me,
watchful, yet assured by the pacific manner of my
approach. I seated myself on a log—the Indian

followed my example, with an appearance of perfect indifference, while his vigilant eye wandered covertly to my gun, and then to the lodge where his own was deposited. The woman, with a similar expression of apathy in her countenance, threw her glance hastily into the forest, and listened, as if to discover whether other footsteps were approaching. There was a silence for some minutes—all parties were equally jealous, but all assumed the same careless air of indifference. At last the Indian, who spoke English tolerably well, said,

" Is the white man hungry?"

I replied, " No."

" Does the white man require a cup of water?"

" I am not thirsty."

" Is the white hunter seeking for a place to sleep? There is my lodge, and the night is coming."

" I am not tired, and I never rest in a wigwam; when I sleep, the earth is my bed and the heavens my covering; I am not a fox, to hide myself in a hole."

" The white stranger is wise," said the Indian with a mock gravity.

" I come," said I, " with the words of peace in my mouth—I wish to hold council with a friend."

" It is not usual for friends to talk together, when one of them holds a gun in his hand."

I took the hint, and laid down my rifle.

" Let us smoke," said I, " I have something of great importance to say."

The Indian made a sign to his wife, who went into the lodge and brought a pipe. It was lighted; each smoked a few whiffs in silence, and passed it gravely to the other.

I now enquired into the lineage of the female, who had so much interested me, but found both herself and her husband very unwilling to communicate any intelligence on the subject. They affected to misunderstand my questions, and gave vague and cold replies. Determined to unveil the mystery, I threw off all reserve, told them I had lost a sister, and repeated some of the circumstances of her capture. They listened attentively, and the woman became interested. They admitted that she had been stolen from the whites when a child, but at first disclaimed all knowledge of any of the facts. At length the woman, giving way to her curiosity, which became excited, began to repeat some reminiscences which she said remained dimly impressed on her mind. She thought she remembered a little boy that used to play with her, and repeated some circumstances which I well recollected. She distinctly remembered that she was playing with her little brother near a small stream, in a valley, when the Indians seized her and carried her away. Other facts were related, which had been gathered from the In-

dians who composed the party—such as the burning of the house, and the capture and escape of
the mother—and it was rendered certain that I
had found my long lost sister! The recognition
was mutual; all parties being satisfied that we
were indeed the children of the same parents.

This conversation lasted until night, when I declined an invitation to sleep in the lodge, and set
out in a direction towards home; but no sooner
was I out of sight of the Indian camp, than I made
a circuit through the woods, and having reached
a spot directly opposite to the course on which I
started, prepared to rest until morning. Such
was my habitual caution, and such my distrust of
an Indian, even though married to my sister.

Early in the morning I sought their camp.
They were not surprised to see me—having understood, and no doubt applauded, the caution which
induced me to lodge apart from them. We break-
fasted together; and my sister conversed with me
more freely than before. The Indians had treated
her kindly, and she was satisfied with her condition. When I asked her if she was happy, she
cast an enquiring glance at her husband, and
shook her head, as if she did not understand the
question. I desired to know if her husband
treated her kindly, when she replied, that he
was a good hunter, and supplied her well with
food,—that he seldom got drunk, and had never

beaten her but once, when, she had no doubt, she deserved it; to which the husband added, that she behaved so well as to require but little correction. As the restraint, caused by my presence, began to wear away, and I was left to converse with her more freely, I invited her to forsake her savage companion, to place herself under my protection, and to resume the habits of civilised life. She received my proposition coldly, and declined it with a slight smile of contempt.

The whole interview was painful and embarrassing. I could not look at the Indian husband of my sister without aversion, and her children, with their wild dark eyes, and savage features, were to me objects of inexpressible loathing. Between my sister and myself there were no points of sympathy, no common attachments, nothing to bind us by any tie of affection or esteem, or to render the society of either agreeable to the other. The bond of consanguinity becomes a feeble and tuneless chord, when it ceases to unite hearts which throb in unison; like the loosened and detached string of a musical instrument, it has no melody in itself, but only yields its delightful notes when attuned in harmony with the other various affections of the heart. There had been a time, when the name of *sister* was music to my ear, when it was surrounded with tender and romantic associations,

and when it called up those mingled emotions of
love, respect, and gallantry, with which we regard
a cherished female relative. But I had seen her,
and the illusion was destroyed. Instead of the
lovely woman, endued with the appropriate graces
of her sex, I found her in the garb of the wilderness, the voluntary companion of a savage, the
mother of squalid imps, who were destined to a
life of rapine; instead of a gentle and rational
being, I saw her coarse, sunburned, and ignorant
—without sensibility, without feminine pride, and
with scarcely a perception of the moral distinctions between right and wrong. I left her. We
parted as we had met, in coldness and suspicion.
She gave me no invitation to repeat my visit, and
I had secretly resolved never to see her again.

In sorrow did I begin to retrace my steps
towards my own dwelling. Slowly, and under a
sense of deep humiliation, did I wander back to
the habitations of my own people. My heart was
changed. A shadow had fallen upon my spirit,
which gave a new hue to all my feelings. I could
feel that I was an altered man.

I reached the edge of the prairie, and seated
myself upon an elevated spot, under the shade of a
large tree. The wide lawn was spread before me,
glowing with the beams of the noon-day sun. A
gentle breeze fanned my temples that were throbbing with the excitement of deep emotion. The

angry passions of my heart were all hushed. The
storm of the soul had ceased to rage. Revenge
was obliterated. The blight of disappointment
had fallen upon me, and withered all the currents
of feeling. The past was a dream—a chaos.
New-born feelings struggled for existence. I pronounced my sister's name, and burst into tears.

How grateful it is to weep when the heart is
oppressed! How soothing is that gush of tenderness, which, as it pours itself out, seems to relieve
the bursting fountains of sensibility, and to draw
off a flood of bitterness from the soul!

A more calm and a more wholesome train of
reflection succeeded. I had long cherished a
vision, which one moment had destroyed. In the
place of an infant sister who was lost to me, I had
created the image of an ideal being, who became
invested with all the loveliness which an ardent
fancy could depict—and giving the rein to my
imagination, I had alternately revenged her death,
or had indulged the fond anticipation of meeting
her again, not only in the bloom of womanhood,
but in the possession of those virtues and attractions which give dignity and beauty to the female
character. She had been the companion of my
childish sports; and while I cherished an intense
fondness for my early playmate, could I doubt that
her heart, if still in existence, throbbed with a
responsive feeling? I had seen her, and the illusion

was dispelled. The murderers of our mother and our father had taken her to their bosoms, and her destiny was linked with theirs. She was the wife and mother of savages.

Yes—*my sister*,—she, for whom I would have willingly offered up my life, and whose image had so long been treasured in my memory, was contented, perhaps *happy*, in the embraces of a savage, at the very time when I was lying in ambush by the war-path, or painfully following the trace of the painted warrior, to revenge her supposed wrongs. And she had witnessed from childhood those atrocious rites, the very mention of which causes the white man's blood to curdle with horror, and had grown familiar with scenes of torture and murder,—with the slaughter of the defenceless prisoner, and the shriek of the dying victim. She had assisted in decking her warrior husband for the battle field, and received him to her arms, while the guilty flush of the midnight massacre was still upon his cheek. She had heard him recount his exploits. She had listened to the boastful repetition of his warlike deeds, wherein he spake of the stealthy march towards the habitations of the white man—of the darkness that hung around the settler's cabin—of the silence and repose within—of the sudden onset—of the anguish of that little family, aroused from slumber by the flames curling over their heads, and the

9

yells of savages around them—of the children clinging to their mother, and the wife slaughtered upon her husband's bosom—with all the revolting particulars of those demoniac scenes of carnage. She had been an attentive and an approving auditor, for her husband was the narrator and the hero, and her children were destined to acquire reputation by emulating his achievements.

It was enough to have met her in that hated garb—to have seen her sallow check, her wary eye, and her countenance veiled in the insipid ignorance of an uncivilised woman—to have found her the drudge of an Indian hunter—to have learned that she had forgotten her brother, and become estranged from the people of her blood— but the conviction that she was the willing companion of murderers, the wife of a trained assassin, weighed down my heart with a pang of unutterable anguish.

" But if they were murderers, what was I ?"

I was startled. I looked around ; for it seemed as if a voice had addressed me. But there was no one nigh—no form was to be seen, and not a footstep rustled the grass. It was conscience that asked that question. It was the inward moving of my own spirit. There was nothing around me to suggest it. I looked abroad upon the plain, and all was silent, and beautiful, and bright. The sun was shining in unclouded lustre over the

spacious lawn, the flowers bloomed in gaudy
splendour, the bee was busy, and the bird sang.
The face of nature was reposing in serene beauty,
and every living thing was cheerful, except myself.

And why was I unhappy? A blight had fallen
upon my youth, and every tie that bound me to
my race was severed. True: but others had
been thus bereaved, without becoming thus incur-
ably miserable. They had formed new ties, and
become re-united to humanity by other affections,
while I had refused to be comforted. They had
submitted to the will of God, while I had followed
the devices of my own heart.

These reflections were painful, and I tried to
resume my former train of thought. But conscience had spoken, and no man can hush its
voice. We may wander long in error, the per-
verted mind may grope for years in guilt or in
mistake, but there is a time when that faithful
monitor within, which is ever true, will speak.
That small still voice, which cannot be suppressed,
again and again repeated the appalling question:

"If they are murderers, what are you?"

The difference, I replied, is that between the
aggressor and the injured party. They burned
the home of my childhood, and murdered all my
kindred. I have revenged the wrong. They
made war upon my country, ravaged its borders,

and slew its people. I have struck them in retaliation.

But had *they* suffered no injury? Was it true
that they were the first agressors? I had never
examined this question. Revenge is a poor casu-
ist; and, for the first time in my life, I began to
think it possible, that mutual aggressions had
placed both parties in the wrong, and that either
might justly complain of the aggressions of the
other.

That which gave me the most acute pain, and
which was the immediate cause of the self-accusa-
tory train of reflection into which I had fallen,
was the conviction that nearly my whole life had
been passed in delusion. I had imagined the
death of a sister who was living—I had punished,
as her destroyers, those who had treated her with
kindness—I had spent years in a retaliating warfare, which, so far as she was concerned, was
unjust. I had watched, and fought, and suffered
incredible hardships, for one who neither needed
my interference, claimed my protection, nor was
capable of feeling any gratitude for the sacrifices
which I had made. If, in respect to her, I had
been thus far deluded, might I not have been in
error in regard to other parts of my scheme?
Admitting that it was justifiable to revenge the
murder of my parents, had I not exceeded the
equitable measure of retaliation? It is one of the

strongest arguments against the principle of revenge, that it is directed by no rule, and bounded by no limit. The aggrieved party is the judge of his own wrong, and the executioner of his own sentence; and the measure of recompense is seldom in proportion to the degree of offence.

When once the heart is disturbed by suspicions of its own rectitude, and the work of repentance is commenced, there is no longer any neutral ground upon which it is satisfied to rest. It must smother the suggestions of conscience, or carry them out to complete conviction. Adopting the latter course, I went mournfully home, resolved to study my own heart. Resorting to that sublime code of morals, some of whose precepts had been impressed upon my infant mind by the careful solicitude of a mother, and testing my conduct by its unerring rules, I learned to look back with horror upon the bloody path which I had trod through life; and I determined, by the usefulness of my future years, to endeavour to make some atonement for my former guilty career of crime and passion.

The garb I now wear, and the employment in which you find me, sufficiently explain the result of my reflections, and the extent of my reformation.

9*

THE FRENCH VILLAGE.

On the borders of the Mississippi may be seen the remains of an old French village, which once boasted a numerous population of as happy and as thoughtless souls as ever danced to a violin. If content is wealth, as philosophers would fain persuade us, they were opulent; but they would have been reckoned miserably poor by those who estimate worldly riches by the more popular standard. Their houses were scattered in disorder, like the tents of a wandering tribe, along the margin of a deep bayou, and not far from its confluence with the river, between which and the town was a strip of rich alluvion, covered with a gigantic growth of forest trees. Beyond the bayou was a swamp, which, during the summer heats, was nearly dry, but in the rainy season presented a vast lake of several miles in extent. The whole of this morass was thickly set with cypress, whose interwoven

branches, and close foliage, excluded the sun, and
rendered this as gloomy a spot as the most melancholy poet ever dreamt of. And yet it was not
tenantless—and there were seasons when its dark
recesses were enlivened by notes peculiar to itself.
Here the young Indian, not yet entrusted to wield
the tomahawk, might be seen paddling his light
canoe among the tall weeds, darting his arrows at
the paroquets that chattered among the boughs,
and screaming and laughing with delight as he
stripped their gaudy plumage. Here myriads of
musquitoes filled the air with an incessant hum,
and thousands of frogs attuned their voices in har-
monious concert, as if endeavouring to rival the
sprightly fiddles of their neighbours; and the owl,
peeping out from the hollow of a blasted tree,
screeched forth his wailing note, as if moved by
the terrific energy of grief. From this gloomy
spot, clouds of miasm rolled over the village,
spreading volumes of bile and dyspepsia abroad
upon the land; and sometimes countless multitudes of musquitoes, issuing from the humid
desert, assailed the devoted village with incon-
ceivable fury, threatening to draw from its inhabitants every drop of French blood which yet
circulated in their veins. But these evils by no
means dismayed, or even interrupted the gaiety of
this happy people. When the musquitoes came,
the monsieurs lighted their pipes, and kept up not

only a brisk fire, but a dense smoke, against the
assailants; and when the fever threatened, the
priest, who was also the doctor, flourished his
lancet, the fiddler flourished his bow, and the
happy villagers flourished their heels, and sang,
and laughed, and fairly cheated death, disease,
and the doctor, of patient and of prey.

Beyond the town, on the other side, was an
extensive prairie—a vast unbroken plain of rich
green, embellished with innumerable flowers of
every tint, and whose beautiful surface presented
no other variety than here and there a huge
mound—the venerable monument of departed ages
—or a solitary tree of stinted growth, shattered
by the blast, and pining alone in the gay desert.
The prospect was bounded by a range of tall
bluffs, which overlooked the prairie—covered at
some points with groves of timber, and at others
exhibiting their naked sides, or high, bald peaks,
to the eye of the beholder. Herds of deer might
be seen here at sunrise, slyly retiring to their coverts, after rioting away the night on the rich
pasturage. Here the lowing kine lived, if not in
clover, at least in something equally nutritious;
and here might be seen immense droves of French
ponies, roaming untamed, the common stock of
the village, ready to be reduced to servitude by
any lady or gentleman who chose to take the
trouble.

With their Indian neighbours the inhabitants had maintained a cordial intercourse, which had never yet been interrupted by a single act of aggression on either side. It is worthy of remark, that the French have invariably been more successful in securing the confidence and affection of the Indian tribes than any other nation. Others have had leagues with them, which, for a time, have been faithfully observed; but the French alone have won them to the familiar intercourse of social life, lived with them in the mutual interchange of kindness; and, by treating them as friends and equals, gained their entire confidence. This result, which has been attributed to the sagacious policy of their government, is perhaps more owing to the conciliatory manners of that amiable people, and the absence among them of that insatiable avarice, that boundless ambition, that reckless prodigality of human life, that unprincipled disregard of public and solemn leagues, which, in the conquests of the British and the Spaniards, have marked their footsteps with misery, and blood, and desolation.

This little colony was composed, partly, of emigrants from France, and partly of natives—not Indians—but *bona fide* French, born in America; but preserving their language, their manners, and their agility in dancing, although several generations had passed away since their first settlement.

Here they lived perfectly happy, and well they might—for they enjoyed, to the full extent, those three blessings on which our declaration of independence has laid so much stress—life, liberty, and the pursuit of happiness. Their lives, it is true, were sometimes threatened by the miasm aforesaid; but this was soon ascertained to be an imaginary danger. For whether it was owing to their temperance, or their cheerfulness, or their activity, or to their being acclimated, or to the want of attraction between French people and fever, or to all these together—certain it is, that they were blessed with a degree of health only enjoyed by the most favoured nations. As to liberty, the wild Indian scarcely possessed more; for, although the " grand monarque" had not more loyal subjects in his wide domains, he had never condescended to honour them with a single act of oppression, unless the occasional visits of the commandant could be so called; who sometimes, when levying supplies, called upon the village for its portion, which they always contributed with many protestations of gratitude for the honour conferred on them. And as for happiness, they pursued nothing else. Inverting the usual order, to enjoy life was their daily business, to provide for its wants an occasional labour, sweetened by its brief continuance and its abundant fruit. They had a large body of land around the village, held in parcels by individuals, to whom it was granted by the crown. Most of this was allowed to remain in open pasturage ; but a considerable tract, including the lands of a number of individuals, was inclosed in a single fence, and called the " common field," in which all worked harmoniously, though each cultivated his own acres. They were not an agricultural people, further than the rearing of a few esculents for the table made them such ; relying chiefly on their large herds, and on the produce of the chase, for support. With the Indians they drove an amicable, though not extensive, trade for furs and peltry ; giving them in exchange merchandise and trinkets, which they procured from their countrymen at St. Louis. To the latter place they annually carried their skins, bringing back a fresh supply of goods for barter, together with such articles as their own wants required ; not forgetting a large portion of finery for the ladies, a plentiful supply of rosin and catgut for the fiddler, and liberal presents for his reverence, the priest.

If this village had no other recommendation, it is endeared to my recollection as the birth-place and residence of Monsieur Baptiste Menou, who was one of its principal inhabitants when I first visited it. He was a bachelor of forty, a tall, lank, hard-featured personage, as straight as a ramrod, and almost as thin, with stiff, black hair,

sunken cheeks, and a complexion a tinge darker
than that of the aborigines. His person was remarkably erect, his countenance grave, his gait
deliberate ; and when to all this be added an enor-
mous pair of sable whiskers, it will be admitted
that Mons. Baptiste was no insignificant person.
He had many estimable qualities of mind and
person, which endeared him to his friends, whose
respect was increased by the fact of his having
been a soldier and a traveller. In his youth he
had followed the French commandant in two cam-
paigns ; and not a comrade in the ranks was better
dressed, or cleaner shaved, on parade than Baptiste, who fought, besides, with the characteristic
bravery of the nation to which he owed his lineage.
He acknowledged, however, that war was not as
pleasant a business as is generally supposed. Accustomed to a life totally free from constraint, the
discipline of the camp ill accorded with his desul-
tory habits. He complained of being obliged to
eat, and drink, and sleep, at the call of the drum.
Burnishing a gun, and brushing a coat, and polish-
ing shoes, were duties beneath a gentleman ; and,
after all, Baptiste saw but little honour in tracking
the wily Indians through endless swamps. Besides, he began to have some scruples as to the
propriety of cutting the throats of the respectable
gentry whom he had been in the habit of considering as the original and lawful possessors of the

soil. He therefore proposed to resign, and was
surprised when his commander informed him that
he was enlisted for a term, which was not yet
expired. He bowed, shrugged his shoulders, and
submitted to his fate. He had too much honour
to desert, and was too loyal, and too polite, to
murmur; but he, forthwith, made a solemn vow
to his patron saint, never again to get into a scrape
from which he could not retreat whenever it suited
his convenience. It was thought that he owed
his celibacy, in some measure, to this vow. He
had since accompanied the friendly Indians on
several hunting expeditions, towards the sources
of the Mississippi, and had made a trading voyage
to New Orleans. Thus accomplished, he had
been more than once called upon by the commandant to act as a guide, or an interpreter—
honours which failed not to elicit suitable marks
of respect from his fellow villagers, but which had
not inflated the honest heart of Baptiste with any
unbecoming pride; on the contrary, there was
not a more modest man in the village.

In his habits, he was the most regular of men.
He might be seen at any hour of the day, either
sauntering through the village, or seated in front
of his own door, smoking a large pipe formed of a
piece of buck-horn, curiously hollowed out, and
lined with tin; to which was affixed a short stem
of cane from the neighbouring swamp. This pipe

10

was his inseparable companion; and he evinced
towards it a constancy which would have immor-
talized his name, had it been displayed in a better
cause. When he walked abroad, it was to stroll
leisurely from door to door, chatting familiarly
with his neighbours, patting the white-haired
children on the head, and continuing his lounge
until he had peregrinated the village. His gravity was not a " mysterious carriage of the body
to conceal the defects of the mind," but a consti-
tutional seriousness of aspect, which covered as
happy and as humane a spirit as ever existed. It
was simply a want of sympathy between his muscles and his brains; the former utterly refusing to
express any agreeable sensation which might haply
titillate the organs of the latter. Honest Baptiste
loved a joke, and uttered many and good ones;
but his rigid features refused to smile even at his
own wit—a circumstance which I am the more
particular in mentioning, as it is not common.
He had an orphan niece, whom he had reared
from childhood to maturity,—a lovely girl, of
whose beautiful complexion a poet might say, that
its roses were cushioned upon ermine. A sweeter
flower bloomed not upon the prairie, than Gabrielle
Menou. But as she was never afflicted with weak
nerves, dyspepsia, or consumption, and had but
one avowed lover, whom she treated with uniform
kindness, and married with the consent of all par-

ties, she has no claim to be considered as the
heroine of this history. That station will be
cheerfully awarded, by every sensible reader, to
the more important personage who will be presently introduced.

Across the street, immediately opposite to Mons.
Baptiste, lived Mademoiselle Jeanette Duval, a lady
who resembled him in some respects, but in many
others was his very antipode. Like him, she was
cheerful, and happy, and single—but unlike him,
she was brisk, and fat, and plump. Monsieur was
the very pink of gravity; and Mademoiselle was
blessed with a goodly portion thereof,—but hers
was specific gravity. Her hair was dark, but her
heart was light; and her eyes, though black, were
as brilliant a pair of orbs as ever beamed upon the
dreary solitude of a bachelor's heart. Jeanette's
heels were as light as her heart, and her tongue
as active as her heels; so that, notwithstanding
her rotundity, she was as brisk a Frenchwoman
as ever frisked through the mazes of a cotillion.
To sum her perfections, her complexion was of a
darker olive than the genial sun of France confers
on her brunettes, and her skin was as smooth and
shining as polished mahogany. Her whole household consisted of herself and a female negro servant. A spacious garden, which surrounded her
house, a pony, and a herd of cattle, constituted, in
addition to her personal charms, all the wealth of

this amiable spinster. But with these she was rich, as they supplied her table without adding much to her cares. Her quadrupeds, according to the example set by their superiors, pursued their own happiness, without let or molestation, wherever they could find it—waxing fat or lean, as nature was more or less bountiful in supplying their wants; and when they strayed too far, or when her agricultural labours became too arduous for the feminine strength of herself and her sable assistant, every monsieur of the village was proud of an occasion to serve Mam'selle. And well they might be; for she was the most notable lady in the village, the life of every party, the soul of every frolic. She participated in every festive meeting, and every sad solemnity. Not a neighbour could get up a dance, or get down a dose of bark, without her assistance. If the ball grew dull, Mam'selle bounced on the floor, and infused new spirit into the weary dancers. If the conversation flagged, Jeanette, who occupied a kind of neutral ground between the young and the old, the married and the single, chatted with all, and loosened all tongues. If the girls wished to stroll in the woods, or romp on the prairie, Mam'selle was taken along to keep off the wolves and the rude young men; and, in respect to the latter, she faithfully performed her office by attracting them around her own person. Then she was the best neighbour and the kindest soul! She made the richest soup, the clearest coffee, and the neatest pastry in the village; and, in virtue of her confectionary, was the prime favourite of all the children. Her hospitality was not confined to her own domicil, but found its way, in the shape of sundry savoury viands, to every table in the vicinity. In the sick chamber she was the most assiduous nurse, her step was the lightest, and her voice the most cheerful—so that the priest must inevitably have become jealous of her skill, had it not been for divers plates of rich soup, and bottles of cordial, with which she conciliated his favour, and purchased absolution for these and other offences.

Baptiste and Jeanette were the best of neighbours. He always rose at the dawn, and, after lighting his pipe, sallied forth into the open air, where Jeanette usually made her appearance at the same time; for there was an emulation of long standing between them, which should be the earliest riser.

"Bon jour! Mam'selle Jeanette," was his daily salutation.

"Ah! bon jour! bon jour! Mons. Menou," was her daily reply.

Then, as he gradually approximated the little paling which surrounded her door, he hoped Mam'selle was well this morning; and she reiterated

10*

the kind enquiry, but with increased emphasis.
Then Monsieur enquired after Mam'selle's pony,
and Mam'selle's cow, and her garden, and every
thing appertaining to her, real, personal, and
mixed; and she displayed a corresponding interest in all concerns of her kind neighbour. These
discussions were mutually beneficial. If Mam'-
selle's cattle ailed, or if her pony was guilty of
any impropriety, who so able to advise her as
Mons. Baptiste? and if his plants drooped, or his
poultry died, who so skilful in such matters as
Mam'selle Jeanette? Sometimes Baptiste forgot
his pipe, in the superior interest of the "tête à
tête," and must needs step in to light it at Jeanette's fire, which caused the gossips of the village
to say, that he purposely let his pipe go out, in
order that he might himself go in. But he denied
this; and, indeed, before offering to enter the
dwelling of Mam'selle on such occasions, he usually solicited permission to light his pipe at Jeanette's sparkling eyes—a compliment at which,
although it had been repeated some scores of
times, Mam'selle never failed to laugh and curtsey
with great good humour and good breeding.

It cannot be supposed that a bachelor of so much
discernment could long remain insensible to the
galaxy of charms which centred in the person of
Mam'selle Jeanette; and, accordingly, it was cur-
rently reported that a courtship, of some ten years

standing, had been slyly conducted on his part,
and as cunningly eluded on hers. It was not
averred that Baptiste had actually gone the fearful length of offering his hand, or that Jeanette
had been so imprudent as to discourage, far less
reject, a lover of such respectable pretensions.
But there was thought to exist a strong hankering
on the part of the gentleman, which the lady had
managed so skilfully as to keep his mind in a kind
of equilibrium, like that of the patient animal between the two bundles of hay—so that he would
sometimes halt in the street, midway between the
two cottages, and cast furtive glances, first at the
one, and then at the other, as if weighing the
balance of comfort; while the increased volumes
of smoke, which issued from his mouth, seemed
to argue that the fire of his love had other fuel
than tobacco, and was literally consuming the inward man. The wary spinster was always on the
alert on such occasions, manœuvring like a skilful general according to circumstances. If honest
Baptiste, after such a consultation, turned on his
heel, and retired to his former cautious position at
his own door, Mam'selle rallied all her attractions,
and by a sudden demonstration drew him again
into the field; but if he marched with an embarrassed air towards her gate, she retired into her
castle, or kept shy, and, by able evolutions, avoided
every thing which might bring matters to an issue.

Thus the courtship continued longer than the siege of Troy, and Jeanette maintained her freedom, while Baptiste, with a magnanimity superior to that of Agamemnon, kept his temper, and smoked his pipe in good humour with Jeanette and all the world.

Such was the situation of affairs when I first visited this village, about the time of the cession of Louisiana to the United States. The news of that event had just reached this sequestered spot, and was but indifferently relished. Independently of the national attachment which all men feel, and the French so justly, the inhabitants of this region had reason to prefer, to all others, the government which had afforded them protection without constraining their freedom, or subjecting them to any burthens; and with the kindest feelings towards the Americans, they would willingly have dispensed with any nearer connection than that which already existed. They, however, said little on the subject; and that little was expressive of their cheerful acquiescence in the honour done them by the American people, in buying the country, which the emperor had done them the honour to sell.

It was on the first day of the Carnival that I arrived in the village, about sunset, seeking shelter only for the night, and intending to proceed on my journey in the morning. The notes of the violin,

and the groups of gaily attired people who thronged
the street, attracted my attention, and induced me
to enquire the occasion of this merriment. My
host informed me that a "king ball" was to be
given at the house of a neighbour, adding the
agreeable intimation, that strangers were always
expected to attend without invitation. Young and
ardent, little persuasion was required to induce me
to change my dress, and hasten to the scene of
festivity. The moment I entered the room, I felt
that I was welcome. Not a single look of surprise, not a glance of more than ordinary attention, denoted me as a stranger or an unexpected
guest. The gentlemen nearest the door bowed as
they opened a passage for me through the crowd,
in which for a time I mingled, apparently unno-
ticed. At length a young gentleman, adorned
with a large nosegay, approached me, invited
me to join the dancers, and, after enquiring my
name, introduced me to several females, among
whom I had no difficulty in selecting a graceful
partner. I was passionately fond of dancing, so
that, readily imbibing the joyous spirit of those
around me, I advanced rapidly in their estimation.
The native ease and elegance of the females, reared
in the wilderness and unhacknied in the forms of
society, surprised and delighted me as much as
the amiable frankness of all classes. By and by
the dancing ceased, and four young ladies of ex-

quisite beauty, who had appeared during the evening to assume more consequence than the others,
stood alone on the floor. For a moment their
arch glances wandered over the company who
stood silently around, when one of them, advancing to a young gentleman, led him into the circle,
and, taking a large bouquet from her own bosom,
pinned it upon the left breast of his coat, and pronounced him "KING!" The gentleman kissed his
fair elector, and led her to a seat. Two others
were selected almost at the same moment. The
fourth lady hesitated for an instant, then advancing
to the spot where I stood, presented me her hand,
led me forward, and placed the symbol on my
breast, before I could recover from the surprise
into which the incident had thrown me. I regained my presence of mind, however, in time to
salute my lovely consort; and never did king
enjoy, with more delight, the first fruits of his
elevation—for the beautiful Gabrielle, with whom
I had just danced, and who had so unexpectedly
raised me, as it were, to the purple, was the fresh-
est and fairest flower in this gay assemblage.

This ceremony was soon explained to me. On
the first day of the Carnival, four self-appointed
kings, having selected their queens, give a ball, at
their own proper costs, to the whole village. In
the course of that evening the queens select, in
the manner described, the kings for the ensuing

day, who choose their queens, in turn, by presenting the nosegay and the kiss. This is repeated
every evening in the week;—the kings, for the
time being, giving the ball at their own expense,
and all the inhabitants attending without invitation. On the morning after each ball, the kings
of the preceding evening make small presents to
their late queens, and their temporary alliance is
dissolved. Thus commenced my acquaintance
with Gabrielle Menou, who, if she cost me a few
sleepless nights, amply repaid me in the many
happy hours for which I was indebted to her
friendship.

I remained several weeks at this hospitable village. Few evenings passed without a dance, at
which all were assembled, young and old; the
mothers vying in agility with their daughters,
and the old men setting examples of gallantry to
the young. I accompanied their young men to
the Indian towns, and was hospitably entertained.
I followed them to the chase, and witnessed the
fall of many a noble buck. In their light canoes
I glided over the turbid waters of the Mississippi,
or through the labyrinths of the morass, in pursuit
of water fowl. I visited the mounds, where the
bones of thousands of warriors were mouldering,
overgrown with prairie violets and thousands of
nameless flowers. I saw the mocasin snake bask-
ing in the sun, the elk feeding on the prairie; and

returned to mingle in the amusements of a circle, where, if there was not Parisian elegance, there was more than Parisian cordiality.

Several years passed away before I again visited this country. The jurisdiction of the American government was now extended over this immense region, and its beneficial effects were beginning to be widely disseminated. The roads were crowded with the teams, and herds, and families of emigrants, hastening to the land of promise. Steamboats navigated every stream, the axe was heard in every forest, and the plough broke the sod whose verdure had covered the prairie for ages.

It was sunset when I reached the margin of the prairie on which the village is situated. My horse, wearied with a long day's travel, sprung forward with new vigour when his hoof struck the smooth, firm road which led across the plain. It was a narrow path, winding among the tall grass, now tinged with the mellow hues of autumn. I gazed with delight over the beautiful surface. The mounds and the solitary trees were there, just as I had left them, and they were familiar to my eye as the objects of yesterday. It was eight miles across the prairie, and I had not passed half the distance when night set in. I strained my eyes to catch a glimpse of the village, but two large mounds, and a clump of trees which intervened, defeated my purpose. I thought of

Gabrielle, and Jeanette, and Baptiste, and the priest—the fiddles, dances, and French ponies; and fancied every minute an hour, and every foot a mile, which separated me from scenes and persons so deeply impressed on my imagination.

At length I passed the mounds, and beheld the lights twinkling in the village, now about two miles off, like a brilliant constellation in the horizon. The lights seemed very numerous—I thought they moved, and at last discovered that they were rapidly passing about. "What can be going on in the village?" thought I—then a strain of music met my ear—"they are going to dance," said I, striking my spurs into my jaded nag, "and I shall see all my friends together." But as I drew near a volume of sounds burst upon me, such as defied all conjecture. Fiddles, flutes and tambourines, drums, cow-horns, tin trumpets, and kettles, mingled their discordant notes with a strange accompaniment of laughter, shouts, and singing. This singular concert proceeded from a mob of men and boys who paraded through the streets, preceded by one who blew an immense tin horn, and ever and anon shouted, " Cha-ri-va-ry! Charivary!" to which the mob responded, " Charivary!" I now recollected to have heard of a custom which prevails among the American French, of serenading, at the marriage of a widow or widower, with such a concert as I now witnessed; and I rode

11

towards the crowd, who had halted before a well-known door, to ascertain who were the happy parties.

"Charivary!" shouted the leader.

"Pour qui?" said another voice.

"Pour Mons. Baptiste Menou, il est marié!"

"Avec qui?"

"Avec Mam'selle Jeanette Duval—Charivary!"

"Charivary!" shouted the whole company, and a torrent of music poured from the full band—tin kettles, cow-horns and ail.

The door of the little cabin, whose hospitable threshold I had so often crossed, now opened, and Baptiste made his appearance—the identical, lank, sallow, erect personage, with whom I had parted several years before, with the same pipe in his mouth. His visage was as long and as melancholy as ever, except that there was a slight tinge of triumph in its expression, and a bashful casting down of the eye—reminding one of a conqueror, proud but modest in his glory. He gazed with an embarrassed air at the serenaders, bowed repeatedly, as if conscious that he was the hero of the night, and then exclaimed—

"For what you make this charivary?"

"Charivary!" shouted the mob; and the tin trumpets gave an exquisite flourish.

"Gentlemen!" expostulated the bridegroom, "for why you make this charivary for me? I have never been marry before—and Mam'selle Jeanette has never been marry before!"

Roll went the drum!—cow-horns, kettles, tin trumpets, and fiddles, poured forth volumes of sound, and the mob shouted in unison.

"Gentlemen! pardonnez-moi—" supplicated the distressed Baptiste. "If I understan dis custom, which have long prevail vid us, it is vat I say— ven a gentilman, who has been marry before, shall marry de second time—or ven a lady have de misfortune to loose her husban, and be so happy to marry some odder gentilman, den we make de charivary—but 'tis not so wid Mam'selle Duval and me. Upon my honour we have never been marry before dis time!"

"Why, Baptiste," said one, "you certainly have been married, and have a daughter grown."

"Oh, excuse me, sir! Madame St. Marie is my niece; I have never been so happy to be marry, until Mam'selle Duval have do me dis honneur."

"Well, well! it's all one. If you have not been married, you ought to have been, long ago:—and might have been, if you had said the word."

"Ah, gentilmen, you mistake."

"No, no! there's no mistake about it. Mam'selle Jeanette would have had you ten years ago, if you had asked her."

"You flatter too much," said Baptiste, shrugging his shoulders;—and finding there was no means of avoiding the charivary, he, with great good humour, accepted the serenade, and, according to custom, invited the whole party into his house.

I retired to my former quarters, at the house of an old settler—a little, shrivelled, facetious Frenchman, whom I found in his red flannel night-cap, smoking his pipe, and seated like Jupiter in the midst of clouds of his own creating.

"Merry doings in the village!" said I, after we had shaken hands.

"Eh, bien! Mons. Baptiste is marry to Mam'-selle Jeanette."

"I see the boys are making merry on the occasion."

"Ah, sacré! de dem boy! they have play hell to night."

"Indeed! how so?"

"For make dis charivary—dat is how so, my friend. Dis come for have d' Americain government to rule de countrie. Parbleu! they make charivary for de old maid and de old bachelor!"

I now found that some of the new settlers, who had witnessed this ludicrous ceremony without exactly understanding its application, had been foremost in promoting the present irregular exhibition, in conjunction with a few degenerate French, whose love of fun outstripped their veneration for their ancient usages. The old inhabitants, although they joined in the laugh, were nevertheless not a little scandalised at the innovation. Indeed, they had good reason to be alarmed; for their ancient customs, like their mud-walled cottages, were crumbling to ruins around them, and every day destroyed some vestige of former years.

Upon enquiry, I found that many causes of discontent had combined to embitter the lot of my simple-hearted friends. Their ancient allies, the Indians, had sold their hunting grounds, and their removal deprived the village of its only branch of commerce. Surveyors were busily employed in measuring off the whole country, with the avowed intention, on the part of the government, of converting into private property those beautiful regions which had heretofore been free to all who trod the soil or breathed the air. Portions of it were already thus occupied. Farms and villages were spreading over the country with alarming rapidity, deforming the face of nature, and scaring the elk and the buffalo from their long frequented ranges. Yankees and Kentuckians were pouring in, bringing with them the selfish distinctions and destructive spirit of society. Settlements were planted in the immediate vicinity of the village; and the ancient heritage of the ponies was invaded by the ignoble beasts of the interlopers. Certain pregnant indications of civil degeneration were alive in the land. A county had been established, with

11

a judge, a clerk, and a sheriff; a court-house and
jail were about to be built; two lawyers had
already made a lodgment at the county site; and
a number of justices of the peace, and constables,
were dispersed throughout a small neighbourhood
of not more than fifty miles in extent. A brace
of physicians had floated in with the stream of
population, and several other persons of the same
cloth were seen passing about, brandishing their
lancets in the most hostile manner. The French
argued very reasonably from all these premises—
that a people who brought their own doctors expected to be sick, and that those who commenced
operations in a new country, by providing so many
engines and officers of justice, must certainly intend
to be very wicked and litigious. But when the
new comers went the fearful length of enrolling
them in the militia; when the sheriff, arrayed in
all the terrors of his office, rode into the village,
and summoned them to attend the court as jurors;
when they heard the judge enumerate to the grand
jury the long list of offences which fell within their
cognizance;—these good folks shook their heads,
and declared that this was no longer a country for
them.

From that time the village began to depopulate.
Some of its inhabitants followed the footsteps of
the Indians, and continue, to this day, to trade
between them and the whites—forming a kind of

link between civilised and savage men. A larger
portion, headed by the priest, floated down the
Mississippi, to seek congenial society among the
sugar plantations of their countrymen in the south.
They found a pleasant spot on the margin of a
large bayou, whose placid stream was enlivened
by droves of alligators, sporting their innocent
gambols on its surface. Swamps, extending in
every direction, protected them from further intrusion. Here a new village arose, and a young
generation of French was born, as happy and as
careless as that which is passing away.

Baptiste alone adhered to the soil of his fathers,
and Jeanette, in obedience to her marriage vow,
cleaved to Baptiste. He sometimes talked of following his clan, but when the hour came he could
never summon fortitude to pull up his stakes. He
had passed so many happy years of single blessed-
ness in his own cabin, and had been so long accustomed to view that of Jeanette with a wistful eye,
that they had become necessary to his happiness.
Like other idle bachelors, he had had his day-
dreams, pointing to future enjoyment. He had
been, for years, planning the junction of his domains with those of his fair neighbour; had
arranged how the fences were to intersect, the
fields to be enlarged, and the whole to be managed
by the thrifty economy of his partner. All these
plans were now about to be realised; and he wisely

concluded that he could smoke his pipe, and talk to Jeanette, as comfortably here as elsewhere; and as he had not danced for many years, and Jeanette was growing rather too corpulent for that exercise, he reasoned that even the deprivation of the fiddles and king balls could be borne. Jeanette loved comfort too; but having, besides, a sharp eye for the main chance, was governed by a deeper policy. By a prudent appropriation of her own savings, and those of her husband, she purchased from the emigrants many of the fairest acres in the village, and thus secured an ample property.

A large log house has since been erected in the space between the cottages of Baptiste and Jeanette, which form wings to the main building, and are carefully preserved in remembrance of old times. All the neighbouring houses have fallen down, and a few heaps of rubbish, surrounded by corn fields, show where they stood. All is changed, except the two proprietors, who live here in ease and plenty, exhibiting, in their old age, the same amiable character, which, in early life, won for them the respect and love of their neighbours and of each other.

THE SPY.

A TALE OF THE REVOLUTION.

Although the title which we have chosen for
this volume, would seem to confine us, in the
selection of our scenes, to an imaginary line
which forms the boundary of our settled population, yet, in fact, the limit which it imposes refers
rather to time than place, for ours is a moving
frontier, which is continually upon the advance.
What is now the *border*, has but recently assumed that character, and if we trace back the
history of our country to its earliest period, in
search of the stirring scenes attendant upon a
state of war, we shall find ourselves rapidly travelling towards the shores of the Atlantic. There
has been a point in the history of every state in
the Union, when a portion of its territory was a
wilderness, and a part, at least of its settlements,
subjected to invasion ; and there have been more

recent and longer periods, when every state contained extensive districts which were thinly settled, and but little frequented by strangers, and where all the vicissitudes and adventures of the border life were experienced by the inhabitants. It is this circumstance which renders the whole of our broad empire so rich in materials for the novelist—for every part of it has been the seat of war, or the scene of border conflict, and there is scarcely a spot where some tradition of a romantic character may not be gathered. I hope, therefore, that the following legend will not be considered as inappropriately grouped with the others which form this little collection.

In a secluded neighbourhood, on the banks of the romantic Susquehanna, stands a large old-fashioned brick house, which, at a period previous to the revolutionary war, was a very important mansion, but has now a mean and dilapidated appearance. It was, when erected, the only respectable building in the whole region of country in which it stands, and was thought to be a noble specimen of architectural skill and magnificence. It was surrounded by a very large plantation, appropriated chiefly to the culture of tobacco and corn, and studded in every direction with little cabins inhabited by negroes. A fine garden, an extensive orchard, and a meadow, in which a number of high-bred horses sported their graceful limbs, showed the proprietor to be a gentleman of easy fortune.

He was indeed, as I learned from tradition, a very wealthy and excellent old gentleman. His portrait, which I used to gaze at with admiration in my childhood, still hangs in the ancient hall, and sufficiently denotes the character of the original. It is that of an elderly robust man, with a fine high forehead, and a mild, though firm expression of countenance. One would pronounce him to have been an unsophisticated man, who had mingled but little with the world, but whose natural understanding was strong. He was a grave, taciturn person, of even temper, and of benevolent and hospitable feelings. His eye was remarkably fine—a large blue orb, full of mildness and love—but with a quiet self-command about it, and a dash of something which said that the owner was accustomed to be obeyed. He was dressed in a snuff-coloured suit, of goodly dimensions; the coat single-breasted, and without a collar, and the wrists ornamented with hand-ruffles.

The portrait of the good lady, which hung by that of her lord, exhibited a stately and very beautiful woman, dressed in all the formal finery of that age. Her complexion was delicately fair, her mouth exquisitely sweet, and her eye proud— but whether that pride arose from the consciousness of her own beauty, or of her dominion over

the handsome gentleman whose name she bore, I
cannot, at this distance of time, pretend to determine.   It is whispered, however, that although
Mr. B.—for this designation will serve our present purpose—ruled his dependents with absolute
authority, and influenced the affairs of the neighbourhood, yet Mrs. B. usually carried her points.
I shall not attempt to describe the lady's dress, as
I am unlearned in those matters.   If Mrs. Hale,
or Mrs. Child, or Mrs. Sigourney, or Mrs. Hentz,
or Miss Leslie, or Miss Sedgewick, or Miss Gould,
or any other of the hundred and one Mistresses or
Misses of our country, who

     " Grace this latter age with noble deeds"

in the way of authorship, had the handling of this
delicate subject, it might be treated with ability,
and the fair writer would luxuriate among the
folds and ruffles of that curious specimen of the
ancient costume ; suffice it, however, to say that
the venerable matron in question wore the hoop,
the stays, the close sleeves, and the high head-
dress ornamented with trinkets, which were common, among well-born dames, in those aristocratic
times.   There was altogether, in addition to her
surpassing beauty, an air of pride, a lady-like elegance, and a matronly dignity, about this lady,
which showed that she thought, and had a right
to think, well of herself; and which gave her a

well founded claim to the obedience of her husband, and all others who might choose to submit to her sway.

But to our story. It was during the most stormy period of the revolution, and Squire B.— for he was a magistrate—and Mrs. B. were both stanch whigs. Not " young whigs," nor modern whigs—but the good old republican rebellious whigs of the revolution. They had given two gallant sons to their country, who were then fighting under the banners of Washington; and were training up the remainder of a large progeny in the hatred of tyranny, and the love of independence. The neighbourhood in which they lived was obscure, and thinly settled; there was no public house of any description within many miles; and genteel strangers, who happened to pass along towards night-fall, were generally, on enquiring for lodgings, directed to the house of Squire B., where they were always sure of a cordial reception, and a gratuitous and most hospitable entertainment. So far from considering such a call as an intrusion, this worthy couple deemed it a great compliment; and would have thought themselves slighted, had a reputable stranger visited the neighbourhood without making their house his home. And a most agreeable home it was to a weary wayfarer. There was kindness without bustle, and profusion without any affectation of

12

display. The self-invited guest was treated as an honoured friend, and an invitation to remain another and another day, was usually accorded to him. Indeed, when one of these chance guests happened to be more agreeable than ordinary, the hospitable Marylander never allowed him to depart in less than a week, nor then without a present of a bridle, a saddle, or perhaps a horse.

It was, as we remarked before, during a perilous time of the revolution, when the hearts of our patriot ancestors were filled with doubt and anxiety, that a solitary traveller rode up one evening to the door of Mr. B. Several negro boys ran to meet him; one opened the gate, another took his horse by the bridle, and a third prepared to seize upon his saddlebags. The stranger hesitated, looked cautiously around, and enquired timidly for Mr. B.

"Ole massa in de house, readen he book;" answered one of the young Africans.

"Do you think I can get permission to spend the night here?"

"Oh yes, massa, for sartin. All de quality stops here."

The stranger still paused, and then alighted slowly, and paused again, as if conscious of the awkwardness of intruding without invitation into the house of one to whom he was entirely unknown. The appearance of the portly owner of the mansion, who now presented himself at the

door, seemed to increase his embarrasment, and
he began, rather bashfully, to make the explana-
tions which appeared to be necessary.

" I have ridden far to-day," said he, " I am
tired, and my horse almost broken down—I am
told there is no tavern in the neighbourhood—and
was directed here—but I fear I intrude."

" Glad to see you," interrupted Mr. B. " come,
sir, walk in—the boys will take care of your
horse—you are quite welcome ; do ye hear, boys,
rub down that nag, and feed him well—no apolo-
gies are necessary, sir—make my house your
home, while you stay in the country—come, sir,
walk in"—and so the old gentleman talked on
until he had got his guest fairly housed, stripped
of his overcoat and spurs, and seated by the fire,
on one side of which sat the lady of the house, en-
throned in suitable state, in a high-backed arm
chair, while her consort placed himself in a
cushioned seat in the other corner. A group of
handsome daughters were clustered round the
worthy dame, like the bright satellites of a
brighter planet—seated on low stools, that they
might learn to sit upright without leaning, and
sewing away industriously under the supervision
of the experienced matron. In the back ground,
immediately behind the ladies of the family, sat a
number of neatly dressed negro girls, carding,
knitting, and sewing—in the process of being

trained up in the way that they should go, in order that, when old, they should not depart from it. These were intended for household domestics, or for personal attendants upon the young ladies, and were carefully taught all the thrifty arts of female industry. Not the least remarkable circumstance which was calculated to attract the eye of a stranger, was the scrupulous neatness of the apartment, the stainless purity of the uncarpeted floor, which was as polished, and shining, and almost as slippery, as ice, with other evidences which attested the vigilant administration of an admirable system of internal police.

The arrival of an unexpected guest caused no disturbance in the well regulated household of Mrs. B., whose ample board was always spread with such a profusion of eatables, that the addition of a company of grenadiers, to her already numerous family, would hardly have been an inconvenience. But there were certain little hospitalities requisite for the honour of the house, and to teach the traveller that he was welcome ; the good lady, therefore, very formally laid aside her knitting and retired, while a servant added several logs to the fire. Mr. B. produced a pipe, in which he sometimes indulged, and having filled it with tobacco, presented it to the stranger, who, being a contemner of the poisonous weed, declined smoking ; and the host, for want of something to say,

lighted it for himself. A negro girl now entered
with a basket of apples, fresh from the orchard,
for it was October, and this fine fruit was in its
perfection; and presently the lady of the mansion
made her appearance, followed by a servant bearing upon a waiter a curiously ornamented silver
bowl, filled with toddy, made by her own fair
hands—for no other less dignified personage than
herself was ever permitted to discharge this most
sacred of all the functions of hospitality. Squire
B., as was the invariable custom, approached the
bowl, and having stirred the delicious beverage
with a spoon, tasted it, in order that he might
have an opportunity of complimenting his good
dame, as he called her, and of remarking, with a
wink, that it "was made strong to suit the ladies."
Then taking the bowl in both hands, he presented
it first, with a formal bow, to his lady-wife, who
touched her fair lips to the brim, then to each of
his daughters, beginning with the oldest, who
successively "kissed the bowl," as Goldsmith
hath it, and lastly to the guest, who did ample
honour to its refreshing contents. Such was the
ceremony invariably observed by this worthy
couple, towards their most cherished friends, and
as invariably extended to the stranger who sought
a shelter at their fireside. Such were the primitive and courteous habits of our venerable fore-
fathers and *foremothers*, in those days when there

12*

were no temperance societies, and when a cordial
reception always included a social cup. They had
no newspapers, nor periodicals, neither albums, nor
scrap-books, nor any of the modern devices for de-
stroying the monotony of an idle hour; and the
bowl must have been found an able auxiliary in
dispelling the dullness of a country fireside.

In the meanwhile, the female part of the company were endeavouring to read something of the
stranger's character in his countenance; and as
they were too well-bred to stare him in the face,
adopted the feminine expedient of stealing a
glance occasionally, when his attention was turned
another way. In this hasty perusal they found
more to excite, than to satisfy, their curiosity; for
the person before them possessed a set of features,
in which different emotions were so strangely
blended, as to baffle the penetration of such inex-
perienced observers. He was so young as to
render it doubtful whether he had more than
merely reached the years of manhood. He was
tall and raw-boned; his large ill-shaped limbs
were loosely hung together, and his manners were
awkward. His face was singularly ugly, being a
collection of angular prominences, in which the
chin, nose, cheek-bones, and forehead, seemed
each to be ambitious of obtruding beyond the
other. But it was an intelligent face, with lines
of thought and observation too strongly drawn

upon it to be mistaken. There was, however, about the muscles of the mouth, and the corners of the eye, a lurking expression of humour, which showed itself, particularly when a local phrase, or a word susceptible of a different meaning from that in which it was intended to be used, dropped in his hearing. Under an assumed gravity, and an affected air of unconcern, there was a watchfulness which could not be wholly concealed, though it betrayed itself only in his eye, which rolled suspiciously about, like that of a cur, who, having, contrary to a standing rule of the house, intruded into the parlour, gazes in every face to learn if he is welcome, and watches every movement as if under a sense of danger. Every attempt to draw him into conversation upon subjects connected with the politics or news of the day, was fruitless; he seemed to be entirely ignorant, or stupidly careless, in relation to the principles and the events of the great controversy which agitated the colonies. On other subjects, of less dangerous import, he spoke well and freely, uttering his opinions in brief, pointed, and sententious remarks, sometimes dropping a sly joke, but always relapsing immediately into his gravity; and shortly after a plentiful supper, he begged permission to retire, which was cheerfully accorded by those who began to be weary of vain efforts to entertain one, who seemed determined to commune only with himself.

The next morning the stranger's stiff and jaded
horse was pronounced to be unfit to travel, and he
cheerfully accepted an invitation to spend the remainder of the day with his kind entertainers;
and when, on the following day, his host again
pressed him to remain, he again acquiesced. During all this time he had but little intercourse with
the family. Mrs. B. was provoked at his tacitur-
nity, the young ladies were out of patience with
his want of gallantry, and the worthy squire was
puzzled what to make of him. The man was
quiet and inoffensive, but had not disclosed either
his name, his business, or his destination. He
sallied forth on each morning, and spent the whole
day in roaming about the woods, or along the picturesque borders of the Susquehanna; and when
the negroes happened to encounter him, he was
usually perched on a log, or lying at his length on
the brow of a hill, with a pencil and paper in his
hand. These employments, so different from those
of their young masters, struck the honest blacks
with astonishment; and they failed not to report
what they had seen in the kitchen, from which,
the tale, with suitable exaggerations, soon found
its way to the hall, where the whole family agreed
in opinion that their guest was a most incomprehensible and mysterious person.

When, therefore, on the third morning, he announced his intention to depart, no polite obstacle

was thrown in his way; the worthy squire con-
tenting himself with thanking his guest for the
honour of his visit, and urging him to call again
whenever he should revisit the country.   He took
leave with his characteristic awkwardness, and
was no sooner out of hearing than the whole
family united in pronouncing him a disagreeable,
unsocial, ill-dressed, incomprehensible, ugly, ill-
mannered person, who had no pretensions to the
character of a gentleman.   An hour was spent in
this discussion, when a servant girl came grinning
into the hall with a pair of shabby, black-looking
saddlebags in her hand, which the stranger had
left in his chamber.   Mrs. B. took them in her
hands, wiped her spectacles, and examined them
carefully, while her husband proposed to send a
boy on horseback to restore the property to its
owner.   But Mrs. B. continued to gaze uneasily
at the saddlebags, turning them over, and pressing
them, to ascertain the character of the contents.

"Mr. B.," said she, at length, "as sure as you
live, there are papers in these saddlebags."

"Well, what then?" said the squire composedly.

"You are a magistrate, and this man is a suspicious character."

"What have I to do with his character, my
dear?"

"You are a justice of the peace, a whig, and a
friend to your country—this man is perhaps a spy,

or a bearer of despatches, and it is your duty to
open these saddlebags."

The squire seemed startled, but shook his head.

"Well, my dear," pursued the lady, "you
always think you know best—but how can you
tell that there is not another Arnold plot among
these papers? You know, Mr. B., that you hold
a responsible office."

"I know, too, that I am a gentleman."

"We all know that, my dear."

"And did you ever know a gentleman to rob
the baggage of his guest?"

The lady looked disconcerted, for the last was a
home argument; her pride was even greater than
that of her husband, and her regard for the rites
of hospitality equal to his.

But what could a man be doing with papers in
his saddlebags, unless he was a spy, or some incendiary agent of the royal cause? The fellow
had a hang-dog look, the saddlebags were suspicious in their appearance, and the papers had a
dishonest rustle. There was treason in all his
actions, and tyranny in every tone of his voice.
Even the negroes had noticed that he was a bad
horseman, which was a sure sign of an English-
man,—and that he was mounted on a wretched
nag, which was evidence enough that the animal
was not his own, or else that he was not a gentleman.

The lady turned these matters in her mind, as she tossed the saddlebags about in her hands.

"You may depend upon it, my dear," said she, "that this is a more serious matter than you have any idea of."

"Very likely," replied the worthy man.

"What *shall* we do?" she exclaimed.

"Let one of the boys gallop after the gentleman with his saddlebags," replied the husband, composedly.

"I am surprised at you, Mr. B. You know not what treason may be in them."

"If the devil was in them, or Arnold himself," replied the squire, with more than usual vehemence, "he might stay there for me. The gentleman asked the hospitality of my roof, he came as a friend, and it shall not be said that I treated him as an enemy."

"Then, Mr. B., if you have no objection, I will open them myself."

"None in the world, my dear, if you will take the shame upon yourself."

The worthy lady dropped the penknife with which she was preparing to rip open the seams of the unlucky saddlebags, and asked, "Do you really think it would be wrong?"

"Decidedly so," replied the husband.

At this juncture, the negro girl, who had been prying about the leathern receptacle, discovered that the padlock was unfastened, and pointed out the fact to her mistress, who exclaimed,

"Nay, then, I will see the inside! And as no lock is to be broken, nor any breach committed, we may serve our country, and, at the same time, save the honour of our house."

In a moment, the contents of the travelling convenience were spread on the floor. From one end was produced a scanty wardrobe, consisting of but few articles; from the other, several handfuls of manuscript. The eyes of the worthy lady glistened as the suspicious papers came to light, and her handsome cheek, on which the pencil of time had not yet drawn a wrinkle, was flushed with patriotism and curiosity.

"Now you see, Mr. B.," she exclaimed, with a kind of *wife-ish* exultation, "you see it is well to listen to advice sometimes. Here's a pretty discovery, truly!"

She now proceeded to open one of the manuscripts, which was folded and stitched into the form of a small book, and read aloud, "*one hundred and nineteenth psalm,*"—"dear me, what's all this?" "*The beautiful and pathetic passage which I have selected, my Christian friends, for your edification*"—"Why it's a sermon!"

"The devil can quote scripture, you know, my dear," said the squire, sarcastically,—"perhaps, as your hand is in, you had better examine a little further."

The remainder of the papers seemed to be of a similar character; and the worthy couple were fully satisfied of the clerical vocation of their late visiter, when the lady inquisitor picked up a loose sheet containing a copy of verses.

" A hymn, no doubt," quoth the lady, " which the worthy man has composed in his solitary rambles."

" Read it for our edification," returned the squire.

" Do, mamma !" cried all the girls at once.

So the old lady began :

" Hail, beauteous shade! secure from eye profane,
    Where chaste Diana, with her vestal train"—

Here the door opened, and, to the utter confusion of the whole company, the stranger stood before them. It was a scene for a painter. There sat the lady of the mansion, on a low chair, with the unlucky saddlebags at her feet, and the contents thereof piled up in her lap. Three beautiful girls leaned on the back of her chair, looking eagerly over her shoulder. The head of the family, who sat on the opposite side of the fire, had taken the pipe from his mouth, dropped his elbows upon his knees, and was gazing and listening with as much interest as any of the circle ;

13

while a half dozen young blacks, with eyes and
mouth open, surveyed the scene with surprise. In
the open door stood the stranger, quite as much
embarrassed as any of the party, who, on discovering him, gazed at each other in mute dismay.
The dismal looks of the host and hostess, when
thus caught in the fact, were really pitiable.
They were a virtuous, honourable couple ; above
fear, but keenly sensitive of shame. The lady
was of gentle blood and nurture, and was proud of
herself, her husband, and her family. The gentleman, though he despised, and never practised
the little affectations and stratagems of pride,
valued himself on his gentility, and on never
doing any act beneath the dignity of a gentleman.
This truly respectable pair had travelled through
life together, and neither of them had ever before
had cause to blush for the act of the other ; and
now, when they stood detected in the disgraceful
fact of opening the private papers of a guest, they
were covered with confusion. Squire B. was the
first to recover his composure ; nor did he, like
our great progenitor, attempt to excuse his own
fault by saying "it was the woman." On the
contrary, being a plain spoken man, and a lover of
truth, he at once disclosed the whole of the reasons
which led to this ludicrous procedure, only placing himself in the position which had, in fact, been
occupied by his wife. He alluded to the perilous

state of the country, to the fact that treason had more than once threatened its liberties, to his own duty as a magistrate, and to the suspicious conduct of the stranger—" Considering all these things," continued he, " our guest will not think it strange, that we have pryed a little more curiously into his private concerns, than would, under other circumstances, have become our wonted respect for the rites of hospitality.

" And yet," resumed the old man, " I am grieved particularly that a clergyman should have been treated uncivilly in my house"—for the squire and his dame were pillars of the church, and revered the clergy.

The stranger, happy in recovering his property, most cheerfully admitted that his kind entertainers had acted for the best.

" And now," said the squire, " to complete our reconciliation, I insist on your spending a week or two with us. On Sunday next you shall preach in our church, and in the meanwhile there are several couples to be married, who have been waiting until they could procure the services of a minister."

This invitation the stranger civilly but peremptorily declined, and taking a hasty leave, retreated to his horse.

Mr. B. accompanied him across the little lawn in front of the house, and the stranger, before he mounted, addressed him thus:—"We are now alone, sir, and some explanation is due to you. I am not, as you at first supposed, a spy, but a native born American, as true to my country as any patriot who fights her battles. Neither am I a clergyman, though I confess, to my shame, that I have assumed that character. I am a student, preparing for the profession of law, but the country wants men in her armies; and although I have removed from town to town, and from one neighbourhood to another, I cannot escape the importunity of recruiting officers, or the ridicule of my friends, for not devoting these sturdy limbs of mine to the common cause."

"Really, young man, I cannot see why you wish to evade military duty in such times as these."

"The gifts of Providence are various," said the young man; "Washington was born a soldier, and I was born—a coward!"

The elder gentleman drew back as if he had seen a rattlesnake in his path.

"It is a melancholy truth," resumed the young man; "I have had a liberal education, my talents are thought to be respectable, and I am gifted with a fund of humour which enables me to mimic whatever I see, and to convulse the gravest company with laughter. Yet I am not happy; for the fear of bodily harm is continually before my eyes. I have an instinctive dread of death; the report of a cannon causes me to shudder; war is my abhorrence; I covet fame; but the idea of having a knife drawn across my throat, or a rusty bayonet thrust through my body, curdles every drop of blood in my veins."

"This is an uncommon case."

"It is uncommon, and therefore I bear it with composure; courage is so ordinary a quality, that it is no disgrace to want it. Cowardice is an extraordinary gift, bestowed on susceptible minds, —courage is a quality which man shares with the bull-dog and the tiger. I was born a timid creature, and no reasoning can cure my sensibility of danger, and my abhorrence of death. I shrink at the idea of pain, and suffer anguish in the contemplation of personal exposure."

"But why assume the character of a preacher?"

"Partly because I am willing to serve my country, according to the nature of my gifts; but chiefly, to be exempt from military duty, and safe from danger. My garb protects me from my enemies, as well as from my friends—from that side which would make me a hero, as well as from the others who would hang me up like a dog. To avoid being a soldier, I have become a saint. I go from camp to camp, and preach up rebellion to our troops. I can declaim with fervour about liberty, for I love it; and I can exhort others to fight bravely, for none can talk so big as a coward."

13*

" But what if you fall in with the enemy?"

" To them I preach peace and good will towards
all men—with a secret prayer that they will prac-
tise it especially towards myself. I carry a few
orthodox sermons with me, such as you have seen,
that suit any emergency. Those I make use of
when my auditors belong to the royal party ; and,
if I do them no good, I am sure that I am doing
my country no evil. My patriotic efforts are all
extemporaneous. My ambition does not point to
martyrdom, any more than to military glory, and
I carry no seditious manuscripts. The recent
course of liberal studies, through which I have
passed, has imbued my mind with arguments in
favour of patriotism and military glory. I take
my text from the scripture, my sermon from the
classics. He who would disseminate the gospel of
peace, or promote the happiness of man, must im-
bibe wisdom from the oracles of God ; but for him
whose purpose is to promote bloodshed and per-
petuate war, the elegant productions of enlightened
Greece, and cultivated Rome, afford a copious
stream of reasoning and illustration."

The young man extended his hand to his host,
thanked him heartily for his hospitable treatment,
mounted his horse, and rode slowly away—leaving
the whole family amused and puzzled with the
events of this singular visit.

THE CAPUCHIN.

[There is a tradition preserved among the French of a celebrated missionary of their nation, who was one of the earliest of the explorers of the Mississippi and its tributaries, and who died at some spot which is now unknown. We have endeavoured to preserve some of the circumstances, which are related as having attended his death, in the following lines.]

There is a wild and lonely dell,
 Far in the wooded west,
Where never summer's sunbeam fell
 To break its long lone rest;

Where never blast of winter swept,
 To ruffle, or to chill,
The calm pellucid lake, that slept
 O'erhung with rock an. hill.

A woodland scene by hills enclosed,
 By rocky barriers curbed,
Where shade and silence have reposed
 For ages undisturbed,

Unless when some dark Indian maid,
   Or prophet old and grey,
Have hied them to the solemn shade
   To weep alone, or pray.

For holy rite and gentle love
   Are still so near akin,
They ever choose the sweetest grove
   To pay their homage in.

One morn the boatman's bugle note
   Was heard within the dell,
And o'er the blue wave seemed to float
   Like some unearthly swell.

The boatman's song, the plash of oar,
   The gush of parting wave,
Are faintly heard along the shore,
   And echoed from each cave.

A skiff appears, by rowers stout
   Urged swiftly o'er the tide;
An aged man sat wrapt in thought,
   Who seemed the helm to guide.

He was a holy capuchin,
   Thin locks were on his brow;
His eye, that bright and bold had been,
   With age was darkened now.

From distant lands, beyond the sea,
   The hoary pilgrim came
To combat base idolatry,
   And spread the Holy Name.

From tribe to tribe the good man went,
  The sacred cross he bore;
And savage men, on slaughter bent,
  Would listen and adore.

But worn with age, his mission done,
  Earth had for him no tie,
He had no further wish, save one—
  To hie him home and die.

——"Good father, let us not delay
  Within this gloomy dell;
'Tis here that savage legends say
  Their sinless spirits dwell.

"In every cool sequestered cave
  Of this romantic shore,
The spirits of the fair and brave
  Unite, to part no more.

"Invisible, the light canoe
  They paddle o'er the lake,
Or track the deer in the morning dew,
  Among the tangled brake.

"'Tis said their forms, by moonlight seen,
  Float gently on the air;
But mortal eye has seldom been
  The fearful sight could bear.

"Then, holy father, venture not
  To linger in the dell;
It is a pure and blessed spot,
  Where only spirits dwell.

" The hallowed foot of prophet seer,
  Or pure and spotless maid,
May only dare to wander here
  When night has spread her shade!"

——" Dispel, my son, thy groundless fear,
  And let thy heart be bold;
For see, upon my breast I bear
  The consecrated gold.

" The blessed cross! that long hath been
  Companion of my path—
Preserved me in the tempest's din,
  Or stayed the heathen's wrath—

" Shall guard us still from threatened harm,
  What form soe'er it take:
The hurricane, the savage arm,
  Or spirit of the lake."

——" But, father, shall we never cease
  Through savage wilds to roam?
My heart is yearning for the peace
  That smiles for us at home.

" We've traced the river of the west,
  From sea to fountain head,
And sailed o'er broad Superior's breast,
  By wild adventure led.

" We've slept beneath the cypress' shade,
  Where noisome reptiles lay;
We've chased the panther to his bed,
  And heard the grim wolf bay.

"And now for sunny France we sigh,
  For quiet, and for home ;
Then bid us pass the valley by
  Where only spirits roam."

——"Repine not, son! old age is slow,
  And feeble feet are mine ;
This moment to my home I go,
  And thou shalt go to thine.

"But ere I quit this vale of death,
  For realms more bright and fair,
On yon green shore my feeble breath
  Shall rise to Heaven in prayer.

"Then high on yonder headland's brow
  The holy altar raise ;
Uprear the cross and let us bow,
  With humble heart, in praise."

Thus said, the cross was soon uprear'd
  On that lone heathen shore,
Where never Christian voice was heard
  In prayer to God before.

The old man knelt— his head was bare,
  His arms crossed on his breast ;
He prayed, but none could hear the prayer
  His withered lips expressed.

He ceased—they raised the holy man,
  Then gazed in silent dread ;
Chill through each vein the life-blood ran—
  The pilgrim's soul was fled !

In silence prayed each voyager,
  Their beads they counted o'er,
Then made a hasty sepulchre
  Upon that fatal shore.

Beside the altar where he knelt,
  And where the Lord released
His spirit from its pilgrimage,
  They laid the holy priest.

In fear, in haste, a brief adieu
  The wondering boatmen take,
Then rapidly their course pursue
  Across the haunted lake.

In after years, when bolder men
  The vale of spirits sought,
O'er many a wild and wooded glen
  They roamed, but found it not.

We only know that such a priest
  There was, and thus he fell;
But where his saintly relics rest,
  No living man can tell.

The red man, when he tells the tale,
  Speaks of the wrath that fell
On him that dared an altar raise,
  In the Indian's spirit-dell.

THE SILVER MINE.

A TALE OF MISSOURI.

[For the facts detailed in this story, the author is indebted to a very ingenious friend, now deceased. He has done little else to it than to correct the phraseology so as to render it suitable for publication.]

Some twelve or thirteen years ago, when the good land on the northern frontier of Missouri was beginning to be found out, and the village of Palmyra had been recently *located* on the extreme verge of the settlements of the white men, uncle Moses, who had built his cabin hard by, went into that promising village one day, in hopes of finding a letter from his cousin David, then at Louisville, and to whom he had written to come to Missouri. Three hours' pleasant ride brought him *to town.* He soon found Major Obadiah ——, who had been lately appointed postmaster, and who had such an aversion to confinement, that he appropriated his hat to all the purposes of a post-office —an arrangement by which he complied with the

14

law, requiring him to take special care of all letters and papers committed to his keeping, and the instructions directing him to be always found *in* his office, and, at the same time, enjoyed such locomotive freedom, as permitted him to go hunting or fishing, at his pleasure. He was thus ready at all times, wherever he might be, to answer any call on his department, promptly.

The major, seating himself on the grass, emptied his hat of its contents, and requested uncle Moses to assist him in hunting for his letter: "whenever you come to any that looks dirty and greasy, like these," said he, " just throw them in that pile ; they are all *dead* letters, and I intend to send them off to head quarters, the very next time the post rider comes, for I can't afford to *tote* them any longer, encumbering up *the office* for nothing." Uncle Moses thought that they were at *head* quarters already, but made no remark, and quietly putting on his spectacles, gave his assistance as required.

After a quarter of an hour's careful examination, it was agreed by both, that there was no letter *in the office* for uncle Moses.

"But stop," said the postmaster, as uncle Moses was preparing to mount his horse, "you are a trading character, come let me sell you a lot of goods at wholesale. Willy Wan, the owner, has gone to St. Louis to lay in a fresh supply, and has left me to keep store for him 'til he returns. He had almost sold out, and I hate to be cramped up in a house all day, so I have packed up the whole stock in these two bundles"—hauling them out of his coat pockets.

Uncle Moses looked over them without ever cracking a smile, for it was a grave business. He wiped his spectacles, to examine the whole assortment.

"Here, examine them—calicoes, ribbons, laces, &c. all as good as new—no mistake—I'll take ten dollars in *coon skins* for the whole invoice, which is less than cost, rather than *tote* them any longer."

Uncle Moses was, in truth, a trading character. He belonged to a numerous and respectable class in our country, who are, by courtesy, called farmers; but who, in fact, spend their whole lives in buying and selling. He was *raised* in North Carolina, and had regularly emigrated westwardly, once in every three or four years, until he had passed through Tennessee, Kentucky, and Illinois, to the frontier of Missouri. Nothing ever made him so happy as an offer to buy his farm. The worthy man would snap his fingers, ask a little more than was offered, and at last take what he could get, pack up his moveables at an hour's notice, and push out further back. He was a famous hand at finding good land; and was sure to get a mill-seat, a stone quarry, or a fine spring, which made his tract the best in the country, and himself the happiest man in the world. He worked hard and made good improvements; but no sooner was his cabin built, his fences made, and his family comfortably settled, than he was sure to find that the neighbours were getting too thick around him, the *outlet* for his cattle was circumscribed, and there was a better country somewhere else. He was not a discontented man—far from it. There never was a better tempered old soul than uncle Moses. But he liked money, loved to be moving, and, above all things, gloried in "a good trade." He would buy any thing that was offered *cheap*, and sell any thing for which he could get the value. He never travelled without exchanging his horse, nor visited a neighbour without proposing a speculation.

Of course, the Major's offer of a lot of *store goods*, for less than cost, struck him favourably, and he offered three dozen racoon skins for the whole. "Take them," said the Major—"it is too little—but if Wan does'nt like the trade, I'll pay the balance myself."

"Now," said the postmaster, "let us go down to the river, where Hunt, and *the balance of the boys*, are fishing. We have been holding an election here for the last two days, and as nobody came in to vote to-day, we all concluded to go fishing."

"But what election is it?"

"Why, to elect delegates to form our state constitution."

"I have heard of it, but had forgot it. I am entitled to a vote."

"Certainly you are. Hunt and I are two of the judges. He has taken the poll-books along with him—come along, we will take your vote at the river—just as good as if it was done in town—I hate formalities, and this three days' election—every body could as well do all their voting in one."

Down they went to the river; the judges and clerks were called together, and recorded the first vote that ever uncle Moses gave in Missouri, on the bank of *North river*, a little below where Massie's mill now stands. I like to be particular about matters of importance.

The parties were soon distributed in quietness along the shore, angling for the finny tribe, which sported, unconscious of danger, in the limpid element. Every tongue was silent, and all eyes resting on the lines, when Sam Smoke made his appearance, cracking his way through the bushes. "Mose! come this way," said he. Uncle Moses, discovering something momentous in his air, met him at a respectful distance. "Now, Moses," said the odd old genius, "I know, very well, you

14*

have some notion of *entering** Wolf Harbour. I have *located* that place myself long ago; but I don't believe you know it. I will now let you into a secret that you have been some time hunting for, if you will not enter the land about Wolf Harbour before I get my money from Kentucky. The quarter section, including the big spring, is all I want—the balance is not worth entering—and if I can get that, I shall have all the elbow room I want."

"But what is the secret?" said uncle Moses, anxiously.

"You have been hunting for a silver mine—hav'n't you?"

"I have; do you know where it is?"

"No, I do not; but I have left an Indian in a *swing* that I have just completed for the major's amusement. He will swing himself until my return. He has a piece of the ore, and will show us the place where he found it, for a gallon of whiskey. Now, say I shall have Wolf Harbour, and you may have the silver mine."

"Agreed," said uncle Moses, "and for fear somebody else should take a fancy to it, if you will go home with me, I will loan you the money to pay for it."

"No, I am much obliged to you," said Sam,

---

* Buying from the government.

"all I want, is the *chance*, after my money comes."

Uncle Moses found the Indian, as was expected, and took him home with him, where he found his cousin David, just arrived from Kentucky. "Ah! Davy, my boy, I am glad to see you. I have found, or rather I am about to find, the silver mine that I wrote to you about. See here! this is as pure silver ore as ever was seen. This yellow fellow knows where it is, and is to show it to me in the morning."

"That's very well," said David, "but do you know you will find this fellow here in the morning?"

"No doubt of it. I know too much of the Indian not to know how to manage him. I will give him a taste out of that keg, and let him understand that there is more, and you could not whip him away."

Early the next morning, our miners had every thing ready for the expedition. The best horse was packed with the tools, and provisions enough for several days. The Indian guide was directed to lead the way. He hesitated for a moment, as if deliberating upon the course, and then, having fixed it in his mind, set off on a *bee line* towards the hidden treasure. Uncle Moses and David led the pack-horse, and plodded on foot at a half trot; for that is the gait of an Indian, when he has a journey before him. After about two hours' rough travelling through the woods and thickets, the miners were saluted with an " Ah ! ho ! ah !" from the Indian, who had stopped on the side of a hill a little in advance. " Plentee bel-le good-chomac," said he, holding up a piece of the precious ore, glistening in his hand. " By the wars, Davy," exclaimed uncle Moses, as he walked up and sur- veyed the spot, " this is a pretty good prospect— this looks well, to be sure—a right smart chance of metal, I declare !"

The horse was soon unpacked, coats off, and every thing ready for deeper research. Davy took the pick and shovel, and commenced remov- ing the ground which seemed to cover the vein. Uncle Moses sauntered about to examine the line trees, and discover the number of the section ; and the guide, having fulfilled his part of the bar- gain, was left in full possession of the jug, and in a few minutes, was as happy as if he had millions in store.

Uncle Moses returned in a short time, having traced the lines of the tract, and found David as wet with sweat, as if he had been in the river. "Stop, David," said uncle Moses, " you will kill yourself if you go on at this rate—give me the shovel, and rest awhile—you have blistered your hands already." This was literally true, and is usually the case with the first essay in mining ;

the fascination is so great, that the young miner, continually imagining himself almost in sight of boundless wealth, delves on harder and harder, and exhausts his strength, while his hopes yet remain fresh. Uncle Moses proceeded more systematically, and, in about two hours, uncovered the bright vein. What a glorious sight met their eyes! How were their hearts gladdened by the brilliant success of their enterprise! They paused, and silently contemplated the shining mass, which lay in a perpendicular stratum, several inches in thickness, and extended along the whole length of the opening. Again they resumed their labours, traced the vein into the side of the hill, and satisfied themselves, that, according to uncle Moses' estimate—and he was not slow at a calculation—there was, at least, fifty thousand dollars' worth of pure silver then within their grasp. "That is enough to make us both rich," said David.

"Why, it is better than nothing," replied the old speculator, gravely, and with all the importance of one who felt the inward dignity of a nabob; "yes, it is better than making corn, or trading in store goods—fifty thousand dollars is a clever little sum. But it is nothing to what is coming—nothing to the balance that lies in the bowels of the earth."

Having rested a little from their labour, the

dinner-bag was produced, and they sat down to a
cold luncheon, which Davy pronounced to be the
sweetest morsel he ever ate in his life. "I don't
doubt it," replied uncle Moses; "this is one of
the real enjoyments of this world. And now,
David, since I have made your fortune, I hope
you may so manage it as never to lose your relish
for the substantials, by indulging too much in the
luxuries of life."

"Never fear that," said David; "I have been
raised to industry—I intend to go to the legisla-
ture. It takes less head than any thing else that
I know of, and I never heard of a member losing
his appetite for meat or liquor. But who have we
here?"

"If it aint that old Hibbard and his hungry
gang of tall boys," exclaimed uncle Moses; "he
has been hunting for this very mine for several
months. They have been watching us—they have
a canoe at the river, and will try to be at St. Louis
first to *enter* the land. You are a light rider,
Davy, and there is my horse—I gave a hundred
and fifty dollars for him—better stuff was never
wrapped in a surcingle—fix the saddle, mount him,
and put off."

Davy was soon ready. Uncle Moses slipped a
roll of bank notes in his hand, and the junior partner in the silver mine wrapped them carefully in
a handkerchief, which he bound round his body—

conducting the whole operation with an apparent carelessness, to deceive those who were looking on.

"There is the money," whispered uncle Moses, "and two hundred dollars over, to buy horses if needful. Ride slowly off, as if you were going home, and when out of sight take a *dead aim* for St. Louis. Don't lose any time looking for roads —a road is of no account, no how, when a man is in a hurry. Don't spare horse flesh. We can afford to use up a few nags in securing a silver mine. If any body asks your business, you know what to say—it's nothing to nobody. Buy the land before you sleep. I'll camp here till you return, and keep these wolves off."

David obeyed orders, and was soon on a high prairie of parallel ridges extending southward. He involuntarily stopped and gazed with wonder and delight on the first specimen which his optics had ever beheld, on so large a scale, of Nature's meadows. He was naturally of a sanguine temperament and lively imagination, and enjoyed the scene with a higher relish, from its sudden and unexpected appearance. " It beats all," thought he ; "I'd give a thousand dollars, (an hour before he would have said *a dollar*,) to know who cleared up all this land. The day has been, when thousands of acres of tobacco have been raised on these *old fields*—but who raised it ? When I get the silver mine I'll find it out. Yes, I'll hire a half a dozen Yankee schoolmasters by the job, and pay them in *pigs* of cast silver." The importance of his journey, however, soon compelled him to collect his scattered wits, and exert them in determining his course. His geographical knowledge of this country was very limited, as he had passed up the Mississippi in a keel boat, and knew nothing of the interior. But he was aware that his course ought to be nearly south, and that, as the country was thinly settled, he would in all probability have to pass most of the distance without a road or trace of any kind.

He followed the direction of one of the ridges of the prairie, and travelled rapidly, until his progress was suddenly arrested by a deep stream, about a hundred yards in width, margined on each side with a heavy growth of tall timber. "This must be Salt River," said he. It was too deep to ford, and the only alternative was to swim—a feat he would sooner have attempted at some place where assistance might be had in case of accident. But knowing that the defeat of his enterprise, and certain loss of his expected wealth, awaited him if he did not cross, he screwed up his resolution, and determined to pass or drown in the attempt. His money was placed in his hat, and he plunged in; his horse was of powerful muscle, and bore him safely to the opposite shore.

The sun was gilding the west as he emerged

into another beautiful prairie, carpeted with the
matchless verdure of the season, which extended
further than his vision could reach. The evening
was calm and pleasant; a soft breeze only moving
to fan the sweet perfume of the various flowers
which spotted the plain. Not a cloud was to be
seen. The lark, whistling on the rosin-weed, or
a solitary hawk, circling through the air, now
poised aloft, and now darting, with the swiftness of
an arrow, on the half concealed sparrow below,
were the only moving objects on which to rest the
eye of the traveller. The scene was solitary as
it was grand, and naturally led our weary adventurer into a contemplative mood. He thought of
the many instances he had known of the misappli-
cation of the gifts of fortune, and determined, in
his own mind, as he was now heir, apparently, to
a princely estate, that he would use it in such
a manner as to afford the most solid advantages to
himself and his country. He resolved to found
schools for the education of all classes, to make
roads, and to build bridges—especially one over
Salt River. He had a mortal antipathy to the
aristocracy of wealth, and vowed that he would
level the rich down to an equality with the poor;
or, if that should be impracticable, he would level
the poor *up* to the standing of the rich. His fondness for the fair sex induced him to wish to confer

15

happiness on as many of them as possible; but as
it was impracticable, under the present organiza-
tion of society, to confer supreme bliss on more
than *one*, he determined to make one happy
woman, at least, without delay.

At length, night began to drop her curtain
around him, and to stud the skies with her twinkling lamps. The dew rested on the tall grass,
and, as the tops of the latter were sometimes
higher than his horse's back, his own clothes soon
dripped large drops of water. Still he pushed on,
until the weary animal, by often stopping to nip
the green herbage, admonished him that food and
rest are necessary to brute creatures, however
non-essential they may be to the proprietors of
silver mines. But it was not until drowsiness
had so overpowered him that he was several
times on the point of losing his balance, that he
determined to rest for the night. He then dismounted, tied his horse's feet together with the
reins of the bridle, supped on some cold venison
and corn bread, that uncle Moses had put into his
saddlebags, and crawling into a matted hazel
thicket, nestled among the leaves, and slept soundly
until morning.

With the first blush of the dawn, David was
again on his way, somewhat refreshed. But the
wolves having robbed his saddlebags of the remaining provisions, he had nothing wherewith

to break his fast. He jogged on at a pretty rapid gait, however, fully determined to compensate his appetite hereafter, in the most ample manner, for the privation it was now suffering. " Poor devils, that have neither house nor land," said he, " may travel upon empty stomachs, and *camp out* in the bushes at night, but that will not be my case. I intend to have old bacon all the year round ; and let them eat venison who can get nothing better."

About the middle of the afternoon, he stopped at the first cabin he had seen, and enquired of a homespun lady, who appeared at the door, if he could get something for himself and horse to eat. After asking him a dozen questions about " where he was from—where he was going—how the election had gone—whether he thought the *convention* would make this a free or slave state— where he staid last night—and if he *war'nt mighty* tired ?"—she at last told him " to light." She soon had every thing ready, and invited him to " set up" and help himself, remarking " that it was not very good fare, no how, but if she had known of his coming, she would have had something better."

From this place, he found a road leading to St. Charles, where he expected to cross the Missouri. Sleepy and weary, every rod seemed now a mile, and he had not gone far from the cabin, when he stopped a traveller, that he met, to enquire the distance to St. Charles; " thirty miles," was the reply.

After proceeding half a mile further, he fell in with another, who told him it was " fifteen miles"—a boy, to whom he put the same question, replied that " it was a *good little bit*"—and a farmer, a little further on, informed him that the exact distance was " twenty-one miles from the big oak at the foot of his lane."

It was dark, when he concluded, for the last time, that he must certainly be within a short distance of the river ; and, at length, meeting a negro on the brink of a hill, was assured that it was " not no distance at all." He was soon in the village of St. Charles, and had no difficulty in find-ing the ferryman, who refused, positively, to carry him across the river that night. David had too much at stake to be thus delayed. He stormed—threatened to cut off the ears of the boatman—swore he would kick the mud-walled house from over the head of the unaccommodating French-man—and, finally, talked about regulating the whole town.

" Monsieur Kentuck," said the ferryman, " vat make you so dem hangry ? are you in von great big horry ?"

" I am on business of importance—more depends on it than your paltry gumbo town is worth—so, stir yourself, or I'll be shot if I don't make a fuss."

"Very much horry, eh?" replied the Frenchman—a dark, swarthy fellow, with straight, black hair, and an eye which began to flash with an *amiable* expression, resembling that of an enraged wild-cat. "'Spose den you vait for your horry over—mean time, you cut off *ma hear* for keep yoursef warm!"

Davy, finding he was on the wrong scent, changed his tone, said he had no wish to affront *any gentleman*, and enquired, in a soothing tone, *if money* could procure him a passage.

"Ah, Monsieur, now you talk like von gentiman—'spose you pay me five dollar, may be you cross de Missouri—'spose you no pay me dat, you may go sleep on dis side, sacre!"

Davy accepted the terms: the *ferry boat*, consisting of two canoes covered with a platform, was hauled up, the horse carefully placed in the middle, and the *savage river*, which roared and bubbled around them, was soon passed. The ferryman pointed out the road, and in a few hours our impatient Kentuckian was at the door of the receiver of public monies in St. Louis, shouting manfully, "Who keeps house?" Colonel S., the receiver, from an upper window, told him that he could not *enter* the land, nor the land office, that night; it

15*

was positively contrary to all rule—and Davy, much chagrined, was obliged to sneak off to a hotel. In the morning he hied by times to the land office, and found, to his mortification, that the whole section was covered by a New Madrid claim! Excited now to desperation, he declared that he would work the silver mine, *any how*, in spite of big guns and little men—he did'nt *rally* the government a cent—not he—it was *no account*, *no how*—then he jumped up, struck his heels together, and said he was a horse, a steam-boat, an earthquake—and that he and uncle Mose, with a hundred Kentuckians, could take Gibraltar!

Hanging his hat on one side of his head, he strutted out of the office, endeavouring to control his rage, and half inclined to gratify it, by whipping the first man he should meet. Finally, however, he concluded to send an express to uncle Moses, and set out for Kentucky himself, to raise volunteers enough to set the land officers at defiance, nullify the government, and work the silver mine, *vi et armis.* Meeting with Mons. Donja, an old acquaintance who was a silversmith, he exultingly produced a specimen of the precious ore, and asked his opinion of it.

"Vat you call dis?" said the dealer in bright metals.

"Pure silver ore—the real stuff."

"You mistake, sair; dat is no silvare, but be ver good brimstone!"

"Brimstone, the devil!" shouted the enraged adventurer.

"Ah, oui," replied the mechanic, with a shrug, "very good brimstone for diable; suppose you go in my shop, you shall be satisfy."

Davy went, and was soon convinced, by being almost suffocated with the fumes of sulphur.

This was the climax of disappointment; but David was blessed with a sanguine temperament, and, although easily irritated, had the faculty of as easily abandoning a favourite scheme, in favour of some new project; and, after giving a long whistle, he strolled back to the hotel with an air of so much unconcern, that no one would have dreamed that any sinister event had befallen him. "It all comes of trusting too much to uncle Mose," thought he; "the old man used to be as true on the scent of money as an old 'coon dog on a pest trail—but he is barking up the wrong tree this time."

He now ordered his horse. "Sorry to inform you," replied the landlord, "very sorry, sir—but, your horse is dead."

"Dead!"

"Dead as a house log."

"Misfortunes never come single," said David;

and quietly throwing his saddle over his shoulder, he walked off, singing, from Hudibras or some other celebrated poet,

> " He that's rich may ride astraddle,
> But he that's poor must tote his saddle."

THE DARK MAID OF ILLINOIS.

The French, who first explored the wild shores and prolific plains that margin the Mississippi river, and extend along its tributary streams, believed that they had found a terrestrial paradise. Never before was such a desert of flowers presented to the astonished eye of man—never before was there exhibited an expanse so wide, so fertile, so splendidly adorned. If the beauty of this region delighted them, its immensity filled them with astonishment, and awakened the most extravagant expectations. Their warm and sprightly imaginations were easily excited to lively admiration, by scenes so grand, so lovely, and so wild, as those presented in this boundless wilderness of woods and flowers. The great length of the magnificent rivers filled them with amazement; while the reputed wealth, and fancied productions of the country, awakened both avarice and curiosity.

We can scarcely realise the sensations with which they must have wandered over a country so different from any they had ever seen, and have contemplated a landscape so unexpectedly majestic and attractive. The freshness and verdure of new lands, unspoiled and unimpoverished by the hand of cultivation, is in itself delightful. It is pleasing to see the works of nature in their original character, as they came from the creative hand; and that pleasure was here greatly enhanced by the infinite variety, and magnificent extent, of the romantic scenery. The plains seemed as boundless as they were beautiful, and the splendid groves, which diversified the surface of these exquisitely graceful lawns, invested them with a peculiar air of rural elegance.

Delighted with this extensive and fertile region, they roamed far and wide over its boundless prairies, and pushed their little barks into every navigable stream. Their inoffensive manners procured them a favourable reception; their cheerfulness and suavity conciliated even the savage warrior, whose suspicious nature discovered no cause of alarm in the visits of these gay strangers. Divided into small parties, having different objects in view, they pursued their several designs without collision and with little concert. One sought fame, another searched for mines of gold as opulent as those which had enriched the Spaniards in a more southern part of the same continent. One aspired simply to the honour of discovering new lands, another came to collect rare and nondescript specimens of natural curiosities; one travelled to see man in a state of nature, another brought the gospel to the heathen; while, perhaps, a great number roved carelessly among these interesting scenes, indulging an idle curiosity or a mere love of adventure, and seeking no higher gratification than that which the novelty and excitement of the present moment afforded.

Whatever might be their respective views, they were certainly, in one respect, the most successful of adventurers. They traversed these wide plains with impunity. They penetrated far into the interior of the trackless wilderness. Their canoes were seen tracing the meanders of the longest rivers; and these fearless explorers had already found their way into the heart of this immense continent, while other Europeans obtained, with difficulty, a footing upon the sea coast.

Among the earliest who thus came was Pierre Blondo, who, having served a regular apprenticeship to an eminent barber at Paris, had recently commenced the world on his own account, in the character of valet to an excellent Dominican priest, who was about to visit America. The proverb, " like master like man," had little application to this pair—for never were two human beings more

unlike than they. The worthy Dominican was a
gentlemanly and priest-like personage, and Pierre
a very unassuming plebeian. The master was
learned and benevolent,—grave, austere, and self-
denying; the valet was a jolly, rattling madcap,
who, as he never hesitated to grant a favour or a
civility to any human being who asked or needed
it, thought it right to be equally obliging to himself; and neither mortified his own flesh nor his
neighbour's feelings. The priest mourned over
the depravity of the human race, and especially
deprecated the frivolous habits of his countrymen;
the valet not only believed this to be the best of
all possible worlds, but prided himself particularly
in being a native of a country which produces the
best fiddlers, cooks, and barbers, on the habitable
globe. In short, the master was a priest and the
man a hair-dresser; they both loved and endeavoured to improve their species; but the one dealt
with the inner, the other with the outer man;—
one sought to enlighten the dark abyss of the
ignorant heart, while the other sedulously scraped
the superfluities of the visage. Father Francis
was a mysterious, silent, ascetic man; Pierre was
as mercurial and as merry a lad as ever flourished
a pair of scissors.

However they might differ in other respects,
there was one particular in which Father Francis
and his man, Pierre, exactly agreed; namely, in

an ardent desire to explore the streams, the forests, and the prairies of Louisiana. They were allured, it is true, by very different motives. The priest came to spread the gospel among the heathen, to arrest their vices, and to explode their human sacrifices; the valet travelled to see the lion with one horn, the fountain of rejuvenescence, the white-breasted swans, and the dark-skinned girls of Illinois. Pierre's researches into American history had been considerable, and his opportunities for acquiring a knowledge of the new world singularly felicitous. He had shaved gentlemen who had been there—had scraped the very cheeks which were embrowned by the sun of the western Indies, and had held, with secret delight, betwixt his thumb and finger, the identical nostrils that had inhaled the delicious odours of Florida, the land of flowers. He had listened with admiration to their wonderful stories, some of which almost staggered his credulity. He did not doubt the existence of gold mines, in which the pure metal was found in solid masses—the only objection to which was, that they were too large for transportation,—nor of that wonderful pool, in which, if an old man bathed, he lost the decrepitude of age, and regained the bloom of childhood. These things seemed proper enough, and were vouched for by gentlemen who could not be mistaken; yet it seemed to him marvellous, that the birds should be snowy white, and

16

the ladies black; that the men should be beardless, and the lions have horns; and that gold-dust, grapes, and oranges, should grow and glitter in a wilderness, where there were none but wolves and wild men to gather them.

It is proper to state here, in order to prevent any misunderstanding in a matter of so much importance, that, although Pierre was a barber, he was by no means an insignificant person. He was of honest parentage—the son of a very reputable peasant, who lived decently, and brought up his offspring in habits of industry. He had a fine figure and a very prepossessing countenance. His eye was good, his teeth white, and his smile agreeable. He was, in short, a gentleman—on a small scale, and a most excellent person—in his way.

During the passage, Pierre became a favourite with his fellow voyagers. He played the flute, sang merry songs, shaved the sailors gratis, and on Sundays brushed up the captain as fine as a grenadier. He felt so happy himself, that he could not be easy without trying to make every body happy around him. At odd times, when he was unemployed, he amused himself in fancying the adventures that awaited him, the fine sights he should see, and the heaps upon heaps of gold and jewels that he should pick up in the new world. He thought himself a second Columbus, and had no doubt that high honours would be conferred upon him on his return—the king would make him a count or a marquis; and M. Corneille, who was then in the meridian of his fame, would write a play, and tell his exploits in poetry. The prime minister would probably offer him his daughter in marriage—and a cloud passed over the brow of the merry Frenchman as he reflected that it would be proper to make the lady miserable, by refusing the honour of the alliance. " I shall certainly be very much obliged to him," said Pierre, as he sat musing on the forecastle, gazing at a long stream of moonlight that sparkled on the undulating waves; " very much obliged : and I shall never be wanting in gratitude to a nobleman who shall do me so much honour,—but I must decline it; for there is pretty little Annette, that I have promised to marry, and who shall never have reason to weep for my inconstancy. Annette is a very pretty girl, and she loves me dearly. I really think she would break her heart if I should not marry her. Poor girl! she thinks there is no body in the world equal to Pierre—and I have no reason to dispute her judgment. She is neither rich nor noble, but what of that? When I am master of a gold mine, and a marquis of France, I can elevate her to my own rank; and I will hang strings of pearl, and ornaments of solid gold, about her pretty neck, and her slender waist, in such profusion, that the

meanness of her birth will be forgotten in the glitter of her attire." Thus did Pierre enjoy the
luxury of hope, and revel in anticipation upon the
bright prospects that beamed upon his delighted
fancy. The vessel flew rapidly over the waves;
and, after a prosperous voyage, the new world
spread its illimitable shores, its gigantic moun-
tains, and its wooded vales, before the enraptured
eyes of the weary voyagers.

Pierre was in the new world. It was very
much unlike the old one. Yet its great superiority
did not strike him so forcibly as he had expected.
The St. Lawrence was a noble river; its shores
were green, and the trees were larger than any
he had seen in France; but the sunny clime, and
the rich vineyards of his native land were not
there, nor was there the least sign of a gold mine,
or a pearl fishery. Our adventurer, however, was
of a sanguine temperament, and determined to
suspend his judgment, and hope on for a season.

Shortly after their arrival at Montreal, an expedition was concerted to the newly discovered region of the Upper Mississippi, and Father Francis
made his arrangements to accompany the party.
Pierre, who, in the long voyage across the Atlantic, comparatively agreeable as it was, had become
wearied of the confinement and privations incident
to this mode of travelling, looked at the little boats
launched on the St. Lawrence, for the transporta-

tion of the party, with some distrust, and evinced
a considerable deal of reluctance against embarking in a new adventure. In Montreal he had
found some of the luxuries which he enjoyed at
home, and had been deprived of on shipboard.
There were barbers and cooks, to shave and feed
people; and, new as the city was, there was a
monastery and a ball room, in the first of which,
he could be seated in a snug confessional, when
he went to confess his sins to the priest, and in
the other he could dance without knocking his
head against a spar, or running the risk of jump-
ing overboard. Other considerations, however,
weighed against his indolence and love of pleasure.
He longed to discover the fountain of rejuvenescence, to bathe in its renovating waters, and
secure the miraculous gift of perpetual youth.
He panted for the dignity and advantage of being
sole proprietor of a gold mine, and returning to
merry France with a ship load of treasure,—for
the honour of nobility, the pleasure of refusing the
prime minister's daughter, and the pride of making Annette a peeress. Incited by hopes so brilliant, and so remarkably reasonable, the spirit of
adventure was re-animated in his bosom, and he
embarked with newly invigorated alacrity.

They ascended, with much toil, the rapid current of the noble Lawrence, meandering among its
thousand isles, and gazing with delight on its
16*

rocky and luxuriant shores. They coasted the grand and beautiful lakes of the north, enraptured with the freshness and variety of the scenery; and surveyed with amazement, the great cataract, which has been the wonder of succeeding generations. Every night they encamped upon the banks, and the forest rang with the cheerful sounds of merriment. Sometimes they met the Indians, who gazed upon them as superior beings, and either fled in terror, or endeavoured to conciliate them by kindness and hospitality. It was thus that the Europeans were usually received by the natives of this continent, before little jealousies, and occasional aggressions, were fomented, by hasty retaliation, into lasting hatred. Happy would it have been for our country, and for human nature, had the civilised adventurers to the new world conducted themselves in such a manner as to have deepened, and indelibly engraved upon the savage mind, the feelings of profound respect which their first appearance excited.

When they reached the southern end of Lake Michigan, the waters were high, and they floated over the inundated lands, pushing their boats among the trees of the forest, and over the rank herbage of the low prairies of that region, until they found the current, which had set towards the north, began to flow off in the opposite direction, and floated them into a small stream, running

towards the south. Here they halted for some
days to hunt, and repair their boats; and when
they reached the Illinois, a large, but placid river,
one of the noblest tributaries of the Mississippi,
the.flood had subsided, and the waters were flowing quietly within their natural channel, through
the silent forest.

With what emotions of wonder must those ad-
venturous travellers have gazed upon these wild
scenes! How singular must have been their sensations, when they reflected on their distance
from the civilised world, and thought of the immensity of that immeasurable waste that was
spread around them. They had never imagined,
far less witnessed, a desert so blooming or so
extensive. There was a magnificence of beauty
in its prolific vegetation and gorgeous verdure,
and a grandeur in the idea of the boundless extent
of this splendid wilderness, that must have excited
the imagination to speculations of intense interest.

Pierre seemed to awaken to a new existence
when the boats entered upon this beautiful river;
and he felt a thrill of pleasure as he surveyed the
placid stream and its lovely shores. The river,
deep, unobstructed, and clear as crystal, flows
with a current so gentle as to be almost impercep-
tible, while the overhanging trees protect it from
the winds, keeping it as still and inviolate as the
fountain that sleeps in its native cave. The

stately swan sailed upon the mirror that reflected
her downy plumage, and the gaudy paroquet, rich
in green and golden hues, sported among the tall
trees. The tangled grape vines hung in heavy
masses from the boughs, and the wild fruit trees
dipped their limbs in the water. Here and there
the tall bluffs jutted in upon the river, impressing
their gracefully curved outlines upon the clear
blue ground of the sky, and throwing their long
dark shadows upon the water; but most usually, a
rich border of noble forest trees, springing from a
low shore, hung in graceful beauty over the
stream. Sometimes they saw herds of buffalo,
wading in the tide, sometimes the lazy bear, wal-
lowing in the mire, and, occasionally, the slender
deer, standing in the timid attitude of attention;
while every secluded inlet, or shaded cove, was
filled with screaming wild fowl, of an infinite
variety of plumage.

The travellers arrived, at length, at an Indian
village, where they were entertained with great
hospitality. The chief, surrounded by his wise
men, and his warriors, painted in gay colours, and
decked with feathers, symbolical of peace, received
them with public demonstrations of respect; and a
great company, of different ages, and both sexes,
was assembled to gaze at them, and to do them
honour. The hump of the buffalo, the head of
the elk, and the marrowy tail of the beaver, were

dressed for them, with all the skill of aboriginal gourmandism; they were feasted, besides, upon bear's oil, jerked venison, hominy, and delicately roasted puppies; and the juicy steams of these delicious viands, unvitiated by the villanous artificial mixtures of European cookery, were pleasantly blended with the balmy odours of the forest. Father Francis, among other monastic attainments, had acquired a very competent knowledge of the art of good eating, and did ample justice to the generous fare which spread the board of his savage entertainers; but being a reformer of morals, he determined to show his gratitude by delivering before his new friends a homily against intemperance; resolving, at the same time, to improve so favourable an opportunity of suggesting the propriety of seasoning such gross meats with a few wholesome condiments; for, to his taste, the devouring of flesh without salt, pepper, or sauce, was mere cannibalism. Pierre was a reformer, too, and he made up his mind to improve the gastronomic science of his country, whenever he should become a marquis, by adding the buffalo's tongue and hump, and the elk's head, to the luxuries of a Parisian bill of fare. The cooking of puppies he thought an unchristian and dangerous innovation, which might lead to the destruction of some of the most harmless animals in creation, while the addition which it brought to the list of solid edibles, was not worthy of much commendation.

Having feasted the adventurers,· the Indians presented them with feathers, belts, moccasins, and dressed skins ; and the chief, in the profusion of his generosity, offered to Father Francis fifteen beautiful young girls, but the good man, as any prudent man would have done, wisely declined the acceptance of a present that might prove so troublesome.   Pierre thought he would have ordered things differently : he winked, shrugged, hinted, and at last ventured to beg that he might take one of them, at least, to Paris with him, as a curiosity ; but the inexorable priest advised him to carry a swan, a paroquet, a pet buffalo, or a rattlesnake, in preference.   Finally, when that worthy and highly honoured ecclesiastic had been feasted to repletion, and loaded to weariness with deferential civilities, a soft couch of buffalo robes was spread for him, and a number of young girls stood round him, as he reposed, fanning him with the snowy wings of the swan, and driving away the musquitoes with bunches of gaudy feathers. Pierre thought this a very grand ceremony, and quite comfortable withal ; and determined, that, whenever he should become proprietor of a gold mine, he would enjoy the luxury of slumber with similar attendance.

It would be a question worthy the attention of

the curious in matters relating to the philosophy
of the human mind, whether that love of foreigners
which has ever distinguished the American people,
and made them the sport of every idle traveller
who has chanced to linger on our shores, was not
derived from the aborigines. The vanity of showing off a travelled "lion" at our parties is certainly not original. If it be not an inherent passion in the human breast, it has, at least, prevailed
throughout many ages. The desire to behold the
exotic production of a distant clime—to entertain
one who has roamed through latitudes different
from our own, and had hair breadth 'scapes, has
long been a distinguishing trait in the domestic
manners of our countrymen ; and we are happy
to be able to trace the propensity back to a period
anterior to our existence as a nation. For we do
not set it down among our virtues. Hospitality
may have much to do with keeping it alive, and a
generous love of knowledge may afford it some
nourishment. But we fear that, after all, it rests
upon a solid substratum of vanity, and is cherished
by the oozings of an inquisitive curiosity. The
Illini, however, fared much better in the result of
their attentions to distinguished strangers, than we
who have succeeded and imitated them. They
received the French, with confiding kindness, into
the bosom of their society, and fed them upon the
fat of their land ; and the worthy visiters of that

primitive people recorded their hospitality in terms
of grateful acknowledgment. We have pursued
a similar course of conduct towards other Europeans, and have been sadly traduced and ridiculed
for our pains.

Father Francis took an early occasion to say a
word in season to the savages on the great business
of his mission. They heard him with grave respect, and promised to take the matter into con-
sideration; but, as their intercourse was conducted
entirely by signs, it is not likely that they were
greatly edified. He showed them a telescope, a
mariner's compass, and a watch, and endeavoured
to explain their several properties; they listened
with attention, offered food to the watch, which
they supposed to be a living animal, looked with
fear at the telescope, and picked the old man's
pocket, while he was lecturing upon natural philosophy. Upon the whole, the savages showed
great capabilities for the pursuits of civilised life.
Pierre, in the meanwhile, remained an inactive
spectator of these proceedings. The Indians,
with their usual tact, discovered that he occupied
a subordinate place in the mission, which released
them from the necessity of paying public honours.
But his fine figure, his elastic step, and his open
countenance, won their regard, and obtained for
him the most cordial attention. Though he was
not, as they supposed, a chief, or a prophet, they

imagined that he was a young brave of promise, and perhaps of distinction, in his tribe.

The next morning, the young warriors dispersed themselves in the neighbouring groves, to paint their bodies and decorate their heads. This is one of the most important employments of an Indian's life. No beau, nor dandy, nor exquisite, in any part of the world, expends more time in the laborious duties of the toilet, than is consumed by the savage in decorating his person. Pierre went among them, bowing and smiling, in his usual obliging manner, with his razors, combs, scissors, and pomatums; and, after exhibiting specimens of his skill upon himself, prevailed upon some of his new acquaintances to place themselves under his hands. He was not only a complete adept in his own art, but a man of genius, who could adapt its principles to the circumstances of a new case; and, directed by the slight observations he had been enabled to make, painted up some of the savages, after their own fashion, with peculiar elegance, and to their entire satisfaction. They were delighted with his clever and obliging talents. He exhibited his lancet and tooth-drawers, and explained their use by significant gestures; and the Indians, supposing them to be delicate instruments for torturing prisoners of war, patted him on the head as a valuable auxiliary. He produced a pair of foils, and, while he convinced them that

17

he was a great warrior, caused an infinite deal of
merriment by the contrast of his own dexterity
with the awkwardness of those who were prevailed upon to oppose him.   A pocket mirror, and
some trinkets, which he displayed, won their admiration, and they soon determined, that, although
Father Francis might be highest in rank, Pierre
was by far the greatest man, and most valuable
acquaintance.   Such are the triumphs of genius !
Pierre had ventured upon a delicate experiment,
in which ninety-nine of the most consummately
skilled artists might have failed, where one would
have been successful.

> " There is a tide in the affairs of men,
>   Which, taken at the flood, leads on to fortune ;"

he had touched a fortunate spring, and found. the
talisman which commanded a brilliant destiny.
In the fulness of his heart he opened a small
package of looking-glasses, which he had brought
for traffic, and distributed, them gratuitously
among the warriors, presenting the largest and
most elegant to the chief, who was so much delighted, that he instantly, with princely liberality,
offered him his daughter in marriage.   Happy
Pierre ! he was that day the proudest of men, and
the most blissful of barbers.

Pierre had serious scruples whether he should
accept this generous offer ; not that he considered

it above his merits—on the contrary, he gave the
chief great credit for having had the acuteness to
discover his genius, and the magnanimity to know
how to appreciate it. It was a proposal worthy
of both the parties concerned. But it touched his
honour, while it flattered his pride. He had not
forgotten his obligations to Annette—the merry
dark-eyed girl who had given him the first offering of her young affections. Poor little Annette,
what would she think of it, if he should marry
another lady. He was sure she would never
stand it. The blight of disappointment would
fall upon the warm heart that throbbed so sin-
cerely for him. "No," said he to himself, "I
will be true to Annette, be the consequences what
they may; I have promised her my hand, and a
share in my gold mine; and nothing shall ever
induce me to act in a manner unbecoming a
French gentleman." Having formed this heroic
resolution, he put his hat on one side of his head,
and strutted through the village, with the independent air of a man who chooses to do as he
pleases, and the self-satisfied countenance of one
who has adopted a virtuous determination.

But Pierre knew little of the frailty of his own
heart. Few of us are aware of the backslidings
of which we may be guilty when there is a lady
in the case. He began to reflect, that the partner
so liberally tendered to his acceptance, was the

daughter of a king, and that such an alliance was
not to be picked up every day in the woods of the
new world.   He might grow gray before another
sovereign would condescend to invite him into his
family; and, reasoning in his own mind, that the
proposed marriage would make him a prince, and
heir apparent, he began to entertain strong doubts
whether patriotism, and the honour of the French
nation, did not require him to sacrifice his affections to the glory and advantage of giving a king
to the Illini.   Napoleon has since been called
upon to decide a similar question; and Pierre,
though not a great warrior, loved his country and
himself as well as Napoleon.   He reflected further, that the possession of the sovereign power
would be the readiest way to the discovery of the
fountain of rejuvenescence ; the gold mines would
all be his own, and he could send Annette a ship-
load of the precious metal.   Moreover, he had
already discovered, that in the new world it was
the custom for great men to have a plurality of
wives—a custom that seemed to him to be founded
in good sense—and he saw no reason ·why he
should not comply with it, and, with the first
cargo of gold he should send to France, despatch
an invitation to Annette to share his prosperity
and the happiness of his tawny bride.

When our inclinations prompt us strongly to a
particular line of conduct, it is easy to find reasons

enough to turn the scale.   Indeed, it is most usual
to adopt a theory first, and then to seek out arguments to support it.   Pierre could now find a host
of reasons urging him to instant wedlock with the
Illinois maiden.   And not the least were the advantages which would accrue to Father Francis,
to the church, and to the cause of civilisation.
When he should become a prince, he could take
the venerable priest under his patronage, encou-
rage the spread of the true faith, cause his subjects
to be civilised, and induce them to dress like Chris-
tians and feed like rational beings.   He longed,
with all the zeal of a reformer, to see them powder
their hair, and abstain from the savage practice of
eating roasted puppies.

So he determined to marry the lady; and, having thus definitely settled the question, thought it
would be proper to take the advice of his spiritual
guide.   Father Francis was shocked at the bare
mention of the affair.   He admonished Pierre of
the sin of marrying a heathen, and of the wicked-
ness of breaking his plighted faith; and assured
him, in advance, that such misconduct would bring
down upon him the severe displeasure of the
church.   Pierre thanked him with the most humble appearance of conviction, and forthwith proceeded to gratify his own inclination—believing
that, in the affair of wedlock, he knew what was
for his own good quite as well as a holy monk,

17*

who, to the best of his judgment, could know very
little about the matter.

On the following morning the marriage took
place, with no other ceremony than the delivery
of the bride into the hands of her future husband.
Pierre was as happy as bridegrooms usually are—
for his companion was a slender, pretty girl, with
a mild black eye and an agreeable countenance.
They were conducted to a wigwam, and installed
at once into the offices of husband and wife, and
into the possession of their future mansion. The
females of the village assembled, and practised a
good many jokes at the expense of the young
couple; and Pierre, as well to get rid of these as
to improve the earliest opportunity of examining
into the mineral treasures of the country, endeavoured, by signs, to invite his partner to a stroll
—intimating, at the same time, that he would be
infinitely obliged to her if she would have the
politeness to show him a gold mine or two. The
girl signified her acquiescence, and presently stole
away through the forest, followed by the ena-
moured hair-dresser.

As soon as they were out of sight of the village,
Pierre offered her his arm, but the arch girl darted
away, laughing, and shaking her black tresses,
which streamed in the air behind her, as she
leaped over the logs and glided through the thickets. Pierre liked her none the less for this evi-

dence of coquetry, but gaily pursued his beautiful
bride, for whom he began to feel the highest
admiration. Her figure was exquisitely moulded,
and the exercise in which she was now engaged
displayed its gracefulness to the greatest advantage. There was a novelty, too, in the adventure,
which pleased the gay-hearted Frenchman; and
away they ran, mutually amused and mutually
satisfied with each other.

Pierre was an active young fellow, and, for a
while, followed the beautiful savage with a credit-
able degree of speed; but, unaccustomed to the
obstacles which impeded the way, he soon became
fatigued. His companion slackened her pace when
she found him lingering behind; and, when the
thicket was more than usually intricate, kindly
guided him through the most practicable places,
—always, however, keeping out of his reach; and
whenever he mended his pace, or showed an inclination to overtake her, she would dart away,
looking back over her shoulder, laughing, and
coquetting, and inviting him to follow. For a
time this was amusing enough, and quite to the
taste of the merry barber; but the afternoon was
hot, the perspiration flowed copiously, and he
began to doubt the expediency of having to catch
a wife, or win even a gold mine, by the sweat of
his brow—especially in a new country. Adventurers to newly discovered regions expect to get

things easily; the fruits of labour may be found at home.

On they went in this manner, until Pierre, wearied out, was about to give up the pursuit of his light-heeled bride, when they reached a spot where the ground gradually ascended, until, all at once, they stood upon the edge of an elevated and extensive plain. Our traveller had heretofore obtained partial glimpses of the prairies, but now saw one of these vast plains, for the first time, in its breadth and grandeur. Its surface was gently uneven; and, as he happened to be placed on one of the highest swells, he looked over a boundless expanse, where not a single tree intercepted the prospect or relieved the monotony. He strained his vision forward, but the plain was boundless—marking the curved line of its profile on the far distant horizon. The effect was rendered more striking by the appearance of the setting sun, which had sunk to the level of the farthest edge of the prairie, and seemed like a globe of fire resting upon the ground. Pierre looked around him with admiration. The vast expanse—destitute of trees, covered with tall grass, now dried by the summer's heat, and extending, as it seemed to him, to the western verge of the continent—excited his special wonder. Little versed in geography, he persuaded himself that he had reached the western boundary of the world, and beheld the very spot

where the sun passed over the edge of the great
terrestrial plane. There was no mistake. He
had achieved an adventure worthy the greatest
captain of the age. His form dilated, and his eye
kindled, with a consciousness of his own importance. Columbus had discovered a continent, but
he had travelled to the extreme verge of the
earth's surface, beyond which nothing remained
to be discovered. "Yes," he solemnly exclaimed,
"there is the end of the world! How fortunate
am I to have approached it by daylight, and with
a guide; otherwise, I might have stepped over in
the dark, and have fallen—I know not where!"

The Indian girl had seated herself on the grass,
and was composedly waiting his pleasure, when he
discovered large masses of smoke rolling upward
in the west. He pointed towards this new phenomenon, and endeavoured to obtain some explanation of its meaning; but the bride, if she understood
his enquiry, had no means of reply. There is a
language of looks which is sufficient for the purposes of love. The glance of approving affection
beams expressively from the eye, and finds its way
in silent eloquence to the heart. No doubt that
the pair, whose bridal day we have described, had
already learned, from each other's looks, the con-
fession which they had no other common language
to convey; but the intercourse of signs can go no
further. It is perfectly inadequate to the interpre-

tation of natural phenomena ; and the Indian maid
was unable to explain that singular appearance
which so puzzled her lover. But discovering,
from the direction to which he pointed, that his
curiosity was strongly excited, the obliging girl
rose, and led the way towards the west. They
walked for more than an hour. Pierre insensibly
became grave and silent, and his sympathising
companion unconsciously fell into the same mood.
He had taken her hand, which she now yielded
without reluctance, and they moved slowly, side
by side, over the plain—she with a submissive
and demure air, and he alternately admiring his
beautiful bride, and throwing suspicious glances at
the novel scene around him. The sun had gone
down, the breeze had subsided, and the stillness of
death was hanging over the prairie. Pierre began
to have awful sensations. Though bold and vola-
tile, a something like fear crept over him, and he
would have turned back ; but the pride of a French
gentleman, and a marquis in anticipation, prevented
him. He felt mean—for no man of spirit ever becomes seriously alarmed without feeling a sense
of degradation. There is something so unmanly
in fear, that, although no bosom is entirely proof
against it, we feel ashamed to acknowledge its
influence even to ourselves. Our hero looked forward in terror, yet was too proud to turn back.
Superstition was beginning to throw its misty

visions about his fancy. He had taken a step contrary to the advice of his father confessor, and was in open rebellion against the church; and he began to fear that some evil spirit, under the guise of an Indian maid, was seducing him away to destruction. At all events, he determined not to go much further.

The shades of night had begun to close, when they again ascended one of those elevations which swells so gradually that the traveller scarcely remarks them until he reaches the summit, and beholds, from a commanding eminence, a boundless landscape spread before him. The veil of night, without concealing the scene, rendered it indistinct; the undulations of the surface were no longer perceptible; and the prairie seemed a perfect plain. One phenomenon astonished and perplexed him: before him the prairie was lighted up with a dim but supernatural brilliancy, like that of a distant fire, while behind was the blackness of darkness. An air of solitude reigned over that wild plain, and not a sound relieved the desolation of the scene. A chill crept over him as he gazed around, and not an object met his eye but that dark maid, who stood in mute patience by his side, as waiting his pleasure; but on whose features, as displayed by the uncertain light that glimmered on them, a smile of triumph seemed to play. He looked again, and the horizon gleamed

brighter and brighter, until a fiery redness rose
above its dark outline, while heavy, slow moving,
masses of cloud curled upward above it. It was
evidently the intense reflection, and the volumi-
nous smoke, of a vast fire. In another moment
the blaze itself appeared, first shooting up at one
spot, and then at another, and advancing, until
the whole line of horizon was clothed with flames,
that rolled around, and curled, and dashed upward,
like the angry waves of a burning ocean. The
simple Frenchman had never heard of the fires
that sweep over our wide prairies in the autumn,
nor did it enter into his head that a natural cause
could produce an effect so terrific. The whole
western horizon was clad in fire, and, as far as the
eye could see, to the right and left, was one vast
conflagration, having the appearance of angry
billows of a fiery liquid, dashing against each
other, and foaming, and throwing flakes of burning
spray into the air. There was a roaring sound
like that caused by the conflict of waves. A more
terrific sight could scarcely be conceived; nor
was it singular that an unpractised eye should behold in that scene a wide sea of flame, lashed into
fury by some internal commotion.

Pierre could gaze no longer. A sudden horror
thrilled his soul. His worse fears were realised
in the tremendous landscape. He saw before him
the lake of fire prepared for the devil and his

angels. The existence of such a place of punishment he had never doubted ; but, heretofore, it had been a mere dogma of faith, while now it appeared before him in its terrible reality. He thought he could plainly distinguish gigantic black forms dancing in the flames, throwing up their long misshapen arms, and writhing their bodies into fantastic shapes. Uttering a piercing shriek, he turned and fled with the swiftness of an arrow. Fear gave new vigour to the muscles which had before been relaxed with fatigue, and his feet, so lately heavy, now touched the ground with the light and springy tread of the antelope. Yet, to himself, his steps seemed to linger, as if his heels were lead.

The Indian girl clapped her hands and laughed aloud as she pursued him. That laugh, which, at an earlier hour of this eventful day, had enlivened his heart by its joyous tones, now filled him with terror. It seemed the yell of a demon—the triumphant scream of hellish delight over the downfall of his soul. The dark maid of Illinois, so lately an object of love, became, to his distempered fancy, a minister of vengeance—a fallen angel sent to tempt him to destruction. A supernatural strength and swiftness gave wings to his flight, as he bounded away with the speed of the ostrich of the desert ; but he seemed, to himself, to crawl sluggishly, and, whenever he cast a

18

glance behind, that mysterious girl of the prairie
was laughing at his heels. He tried to invoke
the saints, but, alas! in the confusion of his mind,
he could not recollect the names of more than
half a dozen, nor determine which was the most
suitable one to be called upon in such an anoma-
lous case. Arrived at the forest, he dashed headlong through its tangled thickets. Neither the
darkness, or any obstacle, checked his career; but
scrambling over fallen timber, tearing through
copse and briar, he held his way, bruised and
bleeding, through the forest. At last he reached
the village, staggered into a lodge which happened to be unoccupied, and sunk down insensible.

The sun was just rising above the eastern horizon when Pierre awoke. The Indian maid was
bending over him with looks of tender solicitude.
She had nursed him through the silent watches of
the night, had pillowed his head upon the soft plumage of the swan, and covered him with robes of
the finest fur. She had watched his dreamy sleep
through the long hours, when all others were
sleeping, and no eye witnessed her assiduous care
—had bathed his throbbing temples with water
from the spring, and passed her slender fingers
through his ringlets, with the fondness of a young
and growing affection, until she had soothed the
unconscious object of her tenderness into a calm
repose. It was her first love, and she had given

her heart up to its influence with all the strength,
and all the weakness, of female passion.   Under
other circumstances it might long have remained
concealed in her own bosom, and have gradually
become disclosed by the attentions of her lover, as
the flower opens slowly to the sun.   But she had
been suddenly called to the discharge of the duties
of a wife; and woman, when appealed to by the
charities of life, gives full play to her affections,
pouring out the treasures of her love in liberal
profusion.

But her tenderness was thrown away upon the
slumbering bridegroom, whose unusual excitement,
both of body and mind, had been succeeded by a
profound lethargy.   No sooner did he open his
eyes, than the dreadful images of the night became
again pictured upon his imagination.   Even that
anxious girl, who had hung over him with sleepless solicitude, throughout the night, and still
watched, dejected, by his side, seemed to wear a
malignant aspect, and to triumph in his anguish.
He shrunk from the glance of her eye, as if its
mild lustre would have withered him.   She laid
her hand upon his brow, and he writhed as if a
serpent had crawled over his visage.   The hope
of escape suddenly presented itself to his mind.
He rose, and rushed wildly to the shore.   The
boats were just leaving the bank; his companions
had been grieved at his marriage, and were

alarmed when they found he had left the village ;
but Father Francis, a rigid moralist, and a stern
man, determined not to wait for him a moment,
and the little barks were already shoved into the
stream, when the haggard barber appeared, and
plunged into the water. As he climbed the side
of the nearest boat, he conjured his comrades, in
tones of agony, to fly. Imagining he had discovered some treachery in their new allies, they
obeyed; the oars were plied with vigour, and the
vessels of the white strangers rapidly disappeared
from the eyes of the astonished Illini, who were as
much perplexed by the abrupt departure, as they
had been by the unexpected visit of their eccentric
guests.

Pierre took to his bed, and remained an invalid
during the rest of the voyage. Nor did he set
his foot on shore again in the new world. One
glance at the lake of fire was enough for him, and
he did not, like Orpheus, look back at the infernal
regions from which he had escaped. The party
descended the Mississippi to the gulf of Mexico,
where, finding a ship destined for France, he took
leave of his companions, from whom he had carefully concealed the true cause of his alarm. During the passage across the Atlantic he recovered
his health, and, in some measure, his spirits ; but
he never regained his thirst for adventure, his
ambition to be a marquis, or his desire to seek for

gold. The fountain of rejuvenescence itself had
no charms to allure him back to the dangerous
wildernesses of the far west. On all these subjects
he remained silent as the grave. One would have
supposed that he had escaped the dominions of
Satan under a pledge of secresy.

A new misfortune awaited him at home, where,
to his infinite mortification, he found Annette married to a lank, snivelling pastry cook, dispensing
smiles, and pies, and sugar plums, from behind a
counter, and enjoying as much happiness as she
could have tasted in the rank to which he had
once destined her. It was not kind in her to have
jilted Pierre for a pastry cook, when he would not
have jilted her for any thing less than a princess.
Our hero had stuck to his integrity like a gentleman, until strong temptation overmastered him,
while she had listened to the sugared compliments
of the confectioner, as soon as the back of her
generous lover was turned, and became mistress
of a cake shop, while he was laying plans to make
her a peeress of France, and a princess of Illinois.
Short sighted Annette! to value so slightly the
sincere passion of so munificent a lover! Pierre
received the news of her defection with the composure of a philosopher—shrugged his shoulders,
snapped his fingers, and resumed his humble occupation. He was not the man to break his heart
for a trifle; and, after bearing with fortitude the

18

loss of a gold mine, a throne, and lovely princess,
the infidelity of a light-hearted maiden was not a
thing to grieve over. He lived a barber, and died
a bachelor. When the bloom of youth began to
fade from his cheek, and the acuteness of his sensibilities became a little blunted—when he saw
his rival, the confectioner, prospering and growing
fat, and the prospect of Annette's becoming a
widow, more and more remote, his reserve wore
away, and he began to relate his adventures to his
customers. He became quite celebrated—as all
Europeans are, who have travelled in America—
many flocked to his shop to hear his interesting
recitals, and the burning lake was added, by common fame, to the other wonders of the new world.

The Indian maid followed the white stranger to
the shore, and saw him depart, with grief. She
gazed at the receding boats until they turned an
angle of the river, where they vanished for ever
from her view, and then she sat down, and buried
her face in her hands. Her companions, in sympathy for her feelings, left her alone, and when all
eyes were withdrawn, she gave vent to her feelings,
and wept bitterly over her shame. She had been
betrothed in the face of the whole tribe, and had
been publicly deserted by her lover. He had fled
from her with every appearance of terror and
loathing. She was repudiated under circumstances of notoriety, which deeply wounded her pride;

while a tenderness, newly awakened, and evinced
to the full extent that maiden delicacy permitted,
was cruelly repaid by insult. Nor was the acuteness of these feelings at all blunted by the suspicion that she had been herself an accessory in
producing the melancholy result. Pierre had followed her to the prairie, in all the joyous hilarity
of an ardent lover—he had fled from her in fear,
and, although the cause of his terror was unknown,
she imputed it to something in her own person or
deportment. There is no anguish which a woman
feels so keenly as the pang of mortified affection—
the conviction that her offered love is spurned—
the virgin shame of having betrayed a preference
for one who does not requite it—the mortification
of attempting and failing to kindle the flame of
love. Woman can bear, and thousands have
borne, the pain of loving without being beloved,
when the secret remains hidden in her own bosom;
but when the husband, or the accepted lover, re-
pels, or coldly estimates, the warm and frank
avowal of a virtuous passion, he inflicts a wound
which no surgery can heal, he touches one of the
master springs of the heart, with a rudeness that
reaches its vitality and withers it for ever. Woman can bear pain, or misfortune, with a fortitude
that man may in vain attempt to emulate ; but she
has a heart whose sensibilities require a delicate
observance ;—she submits to power with humility,

to oppression with patience, to the ordinary ca-
lamities of human nature with resignation—nothing breaks her heart but insulted love.

For whole days did the Indian maid wander
through the solitary forest, ashamed to return to
the encampment of her tribe. When led back to
her father's lodge, she avoided the society of the
maiden throng, and fled from the young warriors
who would have courted her smiles. She ceased
to be numbered among the dark-eyed beauties of
her tribe ; and but a few moons had passed away
since the visit of the white strangers from the land
of the rising sun, when a little hillock, on the summit of a lonely mound in the prairie, covered the
remains of the beautiful and love stricken MAID OF
ILLINOIS.

THE NEW MOON.

A TRADITION OF THE OMAWHAWS.

Far up the Missouri river, where the shores of
that turbid stream are bounded by interminable
prairies, the traveller sees the remains of a village
of the Omawhaw Indians. The former inhabitants, obeying a law of their erratic nature, have
removed to some spot still more distant from the
habitations of the white men, and better supplied
with game. Nothing remains of them but those
vestiges which man, however poor or savage,
always leaves behind him, to attest, even in his
simplest state, his superiority over the brute of
the forest.

The ruin is extensive, but of recent date. The
naked poles, that once supported the frail lodges,
are still standing scattered over the plain, and the
blackened embers lie in heaps upon the deserted
fire-places. The area, which was once trodden
hard by human feet, is now covered with a beau-

tiful carpet of short, luxuriant, blue-grass—a production which ever springs up near the habitations
of man, flourishes round his ruined mansion long
after his departure, and clothes with verdure the
grave in which his body reposes. The council-
house, where the warriors met to recount their
victories, or to plan their hostile excursions, is
entirely destroyed, and its remains are only distinguished from those of the other lodges by their
larger size and central situation. Here too is still
seen, crumbling to decay, the post around which
the warriors danced,—where the war-song has
often been sung—where the buffalo-dance has frequently been witnessed—and where perhaps, too,
many an unhappy prisoner has endured the most
dreadful tortures that ingenious hatred could invent.

The village was bounded, on one side, by the
Missouri, whose bold current, discoloured by the
earthy substances with which it loads itself in its
violent career, swept along the foot of the bluff on
which it stood ;—on another, by a deep lagoon, an
expanse of clear water fed by a creek, and filled
with aquatic plants, which shot up luxuriantly
from its oozy bottom. In front a wide prairie,
covered with its verdant and flowery carpet, presented a long undulating line of horizon to the eye.
The whole town was surrounded by a palisade,
now entirely destroyed, beyond which were the
corn fields, where the squaws practised their rude

agriculture, and which furnished a scanty subsistence to this improvident people during the gloom of winter.

The spot has been some time deserted, though hundreds of miles still intervene between it and the most advanced settlement of the whites. For the blight of the white man often precedes him, and the Indian recoils instinctively, even before he has actually suffered by contact with the race which has oppressed his fathers. The shadow of the white man falls before him, and the Indian, chilled by his approach, sorrowfully abandons the graves of his fathers, and seeks a new home in some wilderness less accessible to the footstep of the stranger.

The traveller pauses here to indulge that pensive train of thought, which is always awakened by the sight of the deserted habitations of man. How sacred is the spot which a human being has consecrated by making it his *home!* With what awe do we tread over the deserted threshold, and gaze upon the dilapidated wall! The feeling is the same in kind, however it may differ in degree, whether we survey the crumbling ruins of a castle or the miserable relics of a hamlet. The imagination loves to people the deserted scene, to picture the deeds of its former inhabitants, and to revive the employments of those who now slumber in the tomb. The hearth-stone, which once glowed with

warmth, is cold, and the silence of death is brooding over that spot which was once the seat of
festivity. Here the warrior trod, in the pride of
manhood, arrayed in martial panoply, and bent on
schemes of plunder and revenge. Here stood the
orator and the hoary seer. Here were witnessed
the sports of youth, and the gossip of old age.
The maiden was here in the modest garb of youthful loveliness, listening with downcast eye to the
voice of adulation, or laughing away the hours
with the careless joy of youthful hilarity; the wife
was seen surrounded by the maternal cares, and
the quiet blandishments, of domestic life; and the
child sported in boisterous mirth. Yes—it is the
same feeling;—the wretched wigwam of the poor
Indian was as much his home as the villa of the
Roman senator; and, though the ruins of the one,
from their superior magnificence, may excite more
curiosity than those of the other, the shadow that
rests upon the heart, as we linger among either,
is equally induced by sympathy for the fallen fortunes of those who once flourished and are now no
more. Men are callous to the sufferings of the
living, but few tread with indifference over the
ashes of the dead, or view with insensibility the
relics of ancient days.

All are gone. Some are banished, and others,
as the scripture beautifully expresses it, *are not:*
the graves of the dead may be faintly discerned in

the neglected fields, but the foot-prints of those who have fled to other lands have long vanished from the green sward and the neglected streets. It was thus with Nineveh and Babylon; it was thus with the desecrated seats of the Druids, and with the strong castles of feudal Europe. The story of what they once were lives in song and history; romance has gathered a few fragments, and entwined them with the fabulous creations of genius; but the eye of the spectator, seeking the traces of a vanished reality, finds only the ruins of mouldered edifices, and the ashes of the unconscious dead.

However unsatisfactory may be our researches in such scenes, we linger among them with mournful pleasure. There is something which is remarkably exciting in the contrast between the present and the past. Nothing seizes the imagination so suddenly, or so strongly, as a vivid exhibition of death or desolation contrasted with possession, and life, and loveliness. All, that once was, is gone or is changed. We repose secure, surrounded by solitude and peace, where the warrior once stood at bay, and where danger beat against the ramparts as the waves dash against the rock-bound shore. Where there was life, we stand in the midst of death. The abodes of those who once lived are deserted, and an awful silence prevails.

19

The reptile and the wild beast have taken possession of the spot formerly occupied by the social
circle. The weed and the briar cover the dilapidated hearth-stone, and conceal the long-forgotten
grave. As we gaze at these things, a feeling of
sympathy is awakened in favour of the departed
inhabitant;—however unamiable his character—
however fierce or wicked he may have been, the
blast of desolation has passed over him, and the
heart spontaneously yields its forgiveness to those
sins and errors that have been punished, and the
consequences of which sleep in the tomb with the
aggressor and the victim. And we think of ourselves, and of those who are dear to us. We too
shall sleep—our habitations shall be given to the
stranger, or be swept away by the hand of time;
and the places that knew us once shall know us no
longer, for ever.

We are growing serious. Let us return to the
village. It was, in days past, a pleasant spot, to
those who could find pleasure in the savage state.
The Omawhaws dwelt here for five months in the
year, employed in raising beans and corn for their
subsistence in the winter, and in dressing the buffalo skins which had been taken in the hunt of the
preceding season. During the rest of the year
they wandered over those wide plains where the
buffalo grazes, and the deer and elk are found;
spending the whole time in hunting and feasting

when the game was abundant, and in toil and
starvation when it was not plentiful.

They were often engaged in war. The Saukies,
a warlike tribe, were their enemies, and the fierce
Sioux bands often harassed them. But they continued for years to elude their foes, during the
hunting season, by vigilance, by rapid marches,
and painful retreats; and to defend the village
from assault, by their watchfulness in discovering
the approach of danger, or their courage in repel-
ling it, during the short interval of repose allowed
them while their corn was growing.

Many miles below the town, at a very conspicuous point on the shore of the Missouri, is a
small mound which covers the remains of Wash-
inggahsaba, or the Blackbird, a celebrated chief,
who died some years ago at this spot on his way
home. According to his own wish he was interred
in a sitting posture, on his favourite horse, upon
the summit of a high bluff bank of the Missouri,—
"that he might continue to see the pale faces
ascending the river to trade with the Omawhaws."
A hillock of earth was raised over his remains, on
which food was regularly placed for several years
afterwards. But this rite has been discontinued.
We know not how long a spirit requires to be fed;
but it seems that there is a limit, beyond which it
is not necessary for the living to furnish aliment
to the deceased. A staff supporting a white flag,

that marked to the eye of the distant traveller the
site of this solitary grave, and called for a tribute
of respect to one whom his people delighted to
honour, is no longer in existence.

The Blackbird was a person of singular capacity, and the greatest man of his tribe. He had
an intellect which obtained the mastery of other
minds, and gave him absolute power over those
around him. They honoured his talents, not his
virtues. Though a great, he was a repulsive,
man. He possessed an extraordinary genius,
which enabled him to sway the multitude, and
gain them over to his purposes—but not to win
their affections. They clung to him with devoted
fidelity—followed, served, and obeyed, with a su-
perstitious attachment, which bound them to his
person—but which was not love.

He ruled his tribe with arbitrary power, and
permitted none to share, or to dispute, his authority.
He had gained the reputation of a great medicine
man, who was supposed to wield a mysterious
influence over the lives of those around him, and
the nation stood in awe of him, as the supreme
arbiter of their fate. Whenever he prophesied
the death of an individual, the event ensued with
unerring certainty; and those who counteracted his
views, who disobeyed his counsel, or in any manner incurred his displeasure, were removed agree-
ably to his predictions, and, apparently, by the

operation of his spells. Such a mysterious, dreadful power quelled the wild spirit of the Omawhaw, who stood submissive, awed into silence, in the presence of the despotic chief, and trembled, even in his absence, if a rebellious thought spontaneously swelled his bosom. He was considered as the friend of the Great Spirit; and it was thought that the Omawhaws were particularly honoured, in having such a personage placed at the helm of their affairs. Many were the victims of his ambition. Whenever his keen dark eye fell in displeasure on an individual, and the blighting prophecy was uttered,—the victim, from that instant, bore a charmed life;—he sickened, withered away, and sunk rapidly to the grave. But the power of the chief continued undiminished to the last; and the whites alone believed that they had discovered the dreadful secret of his influence over life and mind—a secret, which even they dared scarcely whisper to each other. Such is arbitrary power,—gained by long years of toil, and held up by painful watchfulness, its harvest is distrust and hatred. Who would be great on such terms?

To the American traders, who were induced, by the enterprising spirit of traffic, to visit that remote region, the crafty chief was probably indebted for his power. It is supposed that they secretly furnished him with the most subtle drugs,

19*

which he used so artfully, that even they who
supplied them, and who thus courted his favour,
by a sacrifice of principle most incredibly atrocious, remained uncertain whether he administered
them directly as poisons, or employed them in the
horrid operations of magic. Certain it is, that
although capricious towards all others, he protected and countenanced the traders with unwa-
vering friendship. He was true to them, and to
the white people in general, under all changes of
fortune or of temper; and there is always reason
to suspect that a mutual kindness of long continuance, between parties so politic and selfish, is produced only by reciprocal advantage. It is said,
that while he compelled the traders to yield up to
him, gratuitously, a portion of their goods, he
obliged his people to purchase the remainder at
double prices, so that the trader lost nothing by
his rapacity.

He delighted in the display of his power, and
seemed, on some occasions, to exert his authority
for no other purpose than to show that he possessed it. One day, during a great national hunt,
in which all the tribe engaged, and which was conducted with the discipline of a warlike expedition,
they arrived, fatigued and thirsty, at the bank of a
fine flowing stream. They had been travelling
over plains exposed to the sun, and destitute of
water, and the sight of a clear rivulet filled the

party with joy. But, although all were parched with thirst, the chief, to their surprise, permitted none to drink, but a white man, who happened to be in company. He gave no reason for his conduct; a cold peremptory mandate announced his will, and a sullen, though implicit, obedience, attested the despotic nature of his command over his submissive followers. The painted warriors, fierce, and wild, and untamed, as they were, neither hesitated nor murmured at an unjust order, which, although it seemed the result of caprice, was probably intended to try their discipline, and to accustom them to obey without question.

There was one that loved him, and towards whom his stern features sometimes relaxed into a smile of kindness. One of our most popular writers—a lady, whose own affections are so pure and refined, as to enable her to describe, with peculiar grace and fidelity, the gentler emotions of the heart—has lately drawn so true a picture of the love of *a father for his daughter*, that I shall not venture "to dwell on this development of affection." Even the callous savage felt it. He, who had no tear nor smile for any other human being, was softened into a feeling akin to love, towards one gentle creature. He had a daughter, called Menae, or *The New Moon*, who was the most beautiful female of the tribe. The Indian women are usually short, and ungraceful; but she had a figure of which an European lady might have been vain. She was taller and fairer than the rest of the Omawhaw maidens, and towered above them as her father did above the men. Her complexion was so light as to be nearly pure, and the blush mantled in her cheek when she spoke. Her figure was beautifully rounded, and her limbs of exquisite proportion. But her superiority was that of stature and womanly grace; she claimed no observance as a tribute to rank, nor made any ostentatious display of her beauty. Her appropriate and euphonous name was given, not merely on account of the mild brilliancy of her charms, but in reference also to the sweetness of disposition, which rendered her an universal favourite, and caused her to be received, at all times, and in every company, with a complacency similar to that with which we welcome the first appearance of the luminary of the night.

Beauty always exerts an influence, for good or evil, upon the female mind. No woman grows to maturity unconscious of a possession, which, if rightly used, is her richest treasure. It is that which raises her above her own sex, and gives her a transcendent mastery over the affections of man. A beautiful woman possesses a power, which, combined with an amiable deportment, and directed by honourable principle, is more efficient than wealth

or genius. No man was ever formed with a heart
so callous as to be insensible to its magic influence. It is a talisman, as potent as the lamp of
Aladdin, in the hands of one who uses it with
modesty and virtue; but a deadly curse in the
possession of a weak or vicious woman.

The destiny of a beautiful girl is most usually
coloured by the possession of this fascinating
treasure. It has a controlling influence upon the
formation of her character, which elevates her
above, or sinks her below, her companions. The
heartless beauty, who lives for conquest, becomes
the most insensible of her sex. Neglecting the
appropriate graces, and solid accomplishments,
which throw so many pure and hallowed fascina-
tions around the sweet companion of man, she
soon learns to feel the want, and to supply the absence, of womanly attractions, by artificial blandishments. Almost unconsciously she becomes
artful, and learns to live in a corrupted atmosphere
of deception. The time soon arrives when the
beautiful flower which attracted admiration withers—and the stem which bore it is found to be
that of a worthless weed.

But where the mind is sound, and the heart
pure, beauty elevates the character of a young
female. The admiration which she receives,
even in childhood, softens her affections, and stimulates her latent ambition. The glance, and the

tone of gallantry, with which she is addressed,
awakens the responsive sentiment which gives the
proper tone to her affections. She feels her
power, and assumes the dignity of her sex. A
womanly tenderness and grace is seen in all her
actions. Accustomed to admiration, her brain is
not turned by the idle breath of unmeaning compliment. Confident in her powers of pleasing, she
rises above the little stratagems, and sordid jealousies, of her sex, and scorns to use any allure-
ment to extort those attentions to which she feels
herself entitled. Thus it is that beauty gives
power to vice, and strength and gracefulness to
virtue.

It is also true, that the possession of beauty is
apt to improve those exterior graces, which are
so important in woman as to be almost virtues,
though, in fact, they involve little moral responsi-
bility. The knowledge that we possess an envi-
able quality stimulates to its improvement. The
woman, who discovers in herself the power of
pleasing, is apt to cultivate that which produces
an effect so gratifying to herself and so agreeable
to others. Her ingenuity is quickened by encou-
ragement. As the man who has a capital to build
upon is more apt to husband his resources, and
aim at great wealth, than him who, having nothing
to begin with, has no expectation of accumulating
a fortune—so the beauty has a capital, which

induces her to study neatness, grace, and propriety.

I know not whether any of this philosophy holds good among the Omawhaws—I am sure that, as things go in our own land, I am not far from the orthodox creed in respect to this delicate matter. Of one thing, however, there is no doubt: Menac was not only the most beautiful of the Omawhaws, but she seemed to feel the consciousness of her advantage, and to improve it with a skill of which the unenlightened heathen around her had no idea. It might have been because she was the daughter of a chief—or because a portion of her father's talents had descended to her—but I am inclined to think it was because she was remarkably handsome. For one or all of these reasons, she was more neat in her dress, more graceful in her carriage, more sedate and modest in her conduct, more dignified, and altogether more lady-like, after the fashion of the Omawhaws, than any other young lady of that nation:—all which I am ready to verify.

Among the Omawhaws, females are usually betrothed in childhood, but the daughter of Blackbird had remained free from any engagement. Great men sometimes trample on national usages which interfere with their own designs, and the politic chief of the Omawhaws might have kept his daughter free from any engagement, in order to

be at full liberty, at any time, to make for her the
best match which his situation might command.
Or, perhaps, the awe in which the chief was held,
and the general belief in his supernatural power,
may have kept the other fathers of the tribe at a
distance, or have induced a doubt in their minds
whether a near alliance with their dreaded leader
was desirable. Such however was the fact. Menac
had now reached her fifteenth year, and the young
warriors began to look towards her as an object of
peculiar attraction. In her presence they reined
up their horses, involuntarily seeking to display
the action of their steeds and their own horse-
manship—or urged their canoes over the eddying
waves of the Missouri with redoubled vigour.
Some of them improved vastly in their attention
to the labours of the toilet, adorned their faces
with an unusual quantity of red paint, and their
necks with the claws of bears—and hung all sorts
of grisly ornaments about their persons. Others
exhibited the scalps of their enemies slain in battle,
with more than ordinary ostentation; and the trophies torn from slaughtered white men became
quite the fashion. But all in vain: the New
Moon moved gracefully in her orbit, shedding
her beams alike on all, and not distinguishing
any with particular marks of her favour.

More than a year previous to the time at which
our tale commences, a young trader had arrived

at the Omawhaw village. Naturally sagacious, and expert in business, he soon became acquainted with the customs of the tribe, and acquired the confidence of the people. His appearance was prepossessing, his look was bold and manly, and his speech prompt and frank, yet cautious and respectful. The squaws called him *the handsome white man*, but the more discriminating warriors designated him *the wise stranger*.

He was one of a very numerous and successful class, who are chiefly distinguished by their faculty for getting along in the world, but who, in consequence of the possession of this one quality, receive credit for many others. Calm, mild, with an agreeable smile always playing over his features, Mr. Bolingbroke was pronounced to be a young gentleman of excellent heart; but the truth was, that his heart had nothing to do with the blandness of his manners. The secret of that uniform self-possession and civility consisted simply in the absence of passion; the heart never concerned itself in Mr. Bolingbroke's business. He was even tempered, because he took no interest in any thing but his own personal advancement; and, as long as his affairs went on prosperously, there was no reason why a perpetual sunshine should not play over his features. He was courteous from policy, because men are managed more easily by kindness than by stratagem or force; and because it was

20

more natural to him to smile than to frown. The
world gave him credit for a great deal of feeling—
simply because he had very little; for the less
sensibility a man has, the more he affects. He
was ardent and energetic in his business, earnest
in the pursuit of pleasure, and gay in company;
but the observer, who had watched him closely,
would have found that the only chords in his
bosom which were ever touched, were those of
self-gratification and self-interest.

The judicious conduct of Mr. Bolingbroke met
its usual reward, and he was prosperous in trade.
But, as time rolled on, other traders came to the
village, competition reduced his gains, and he began to see the necessity of adopting some expedient
which should give him an advantage over his rivals.
This was a matter of too much importance to be
settled in a moment; therefore he studied over it
for several months, smiling and showing his white
teeth all the while, and banishing every shadow of
care from his fine open countenance. He even
squeezed the hands of his competitors more warm-
ly than usual, strolled often to their wigwams,
laughed with glee at their jokes, and seemed
really to love them, and to take an interest in
their prosperity. The result of his cogitations
was a conviction that the most feasible plan for
rising above competition would be that of wedlock,
—that of identifying himself with the tribe, enlist-

ing their affections, and securing the influence of
a powerful friend by a marriage with the daughter
of some influential person; nor did he hesitate a
moment in selecting, as the happy lady, the beauty
of the tribe—the *New Moon*—the only and beloved
daughter of the ruling chief.

The young merchant had more than once looked
with a delighted eye at the graceful form of Menac,
had spoken to her kindly when they met, and had
paid her the homage of gallant courtesy which
beauty always exacts. She had received his attentions with civility, but without any appearance
of being flattered by them. But now her quick
apprehension discovered that there was something
in his manner altogether different from his ordinary politeness. When he met this brightest of
all the stars in the galaxy of Omawhaw beauty,
his eye rested upon her with a peculiar meaning;
and he more than once stopped, as if he would
have spoken. How quick-sighted is woman in the
affairs of the heart! She saw that the white
stranger was smitten; and the conviction afforded
her that mischievous satisfaction, which a pretty
girl always feels, on witnessing the havoc made
by her charms, when her own affections remain
untouched. It was so with Menac; the white
stranger had as yet made no impression on her
heart. Some presents, of more value than those
which he had been in the habit of giving to the

Indian maidens, convinced her of that which she
had begun to suspect; and she whispered to herself, in the exultation of a girl over her first conquest, "the handsome white man loves the New
Moon."

Just at this crisis arrived the season of the grand
summer hunt, when, the corn having been weeded,
the whole tribe abandoned the village, and proceeded to the great plains where the buffaloes
graze in vast herds. This is an occasion of great
rejoicing. For several days previous to the departure of the tribe, feasts were held, and councils
assembled to deliberate on the route, to devise the
plan of the hunt, and to suggest the necessary
precautions to avoid the snares of their enemies.
The elders of the tribe repeated the results of
their experience, the orators embraced the occasion to win new trophies of applause, and while
some were successful in these ambitious attempts,
there were also others who

> "In that unnavigable stream were drowned."

The traders were consulted in reference to the
supply of guns and ammunition; and the hunters
made their contracts individually, in accordance
with which they were provided with rifles, gun-
powder, and other articles, to be paid for in furs
and peltry, at the close of the hunting season.

It was on such occasions, that Bolingbroke had

heretofore discovered his influence to be at its
greatest height among his savage customers; who
treated his suggestions with deference, in proportion to the amount of the favours which they
solicited at his hands. In the wilderness, as in
the marts of civilised life, people are never so
kind to each other as at the moment when the
relation of debtor and creditor is about to be
created, and never less cordial than during the
existence of that obligation. Bolingbroke had
found himself, at one season, worshipped as the
idol of the tribe, and, at another, feared as its
master; but, by being alternately an indulgent
creditor, and an unassuming friend, had retained
its confidence. It was, therefore, with no small
degree of chagrin that he now saw his business
about to be shared, and his influence divided, with
others. His convictions, as to the propriety of
entering into the honourable state of matrimony,
became greatly strengthened by this new evidence
of the evanescent nature of his own popularity;
and his love for the New Moon increased to a
steady flame, as the propitious influence which
this bright star might exert over his fortunes became clearly developed.

The councils continued to be held; and, while
the chief men were employed in maturing the
weighty affairs of their little state, every leisure
interval was filled with sport and feasting. The

20*

men amused themselves with various pastimes,
such as cards, dancing, foot-ball, and racing. The
younger warriors were painted with more than
ordinary care; some gave themselves up to the
affairs of courtship and gallantry—others did
honour to the chiefs and distinguished braves, by
dancing before the doors of their respective lodges
—while a few, ludicrously appareled, moved about
the village, exciting laughter by the performance
of coarse feats of buffoonery. The criers passed
through the streets, inviting individuals by name,
in a loud voice, to feasts given by their friends,
charging them, at the same time, to be careful to
bring their own bowls and spoons; and, again,
proclaiming that the entertainments were over,
praising the hospitality of the several hosts, pub-
lishing the resolves of the council, and admonish-
ing the people to hasten their preparations for
departure.

At length, every requisite arrangement being
complete, the females, to whom the prospect of
such a journey is always gratifying, were seen
moving rapidly about, assiduously occupied in
loading their horses with such moveables as were
necessary to be transported. It was obvious that
they felt their own importance; their active motions, busy faces, and loud talking, evinced that
for the moment they had broken through all the
salutary restraints of discipline, and assumed the

reins of government; and they even ventured to
rate their husbands severely, for real or supposed
trespasses, upon what they considered their peculiar province—as we have understood the ladies of
another tribe, which shall be nameless, are accustomed to do, when their liege lords intrude upon
them while in the performance of any household
solemnities which they regard as inviolate.

The march of the tribe from the village presented a picturesque and beautiful scene. It was
a bright morning in June. The sun was just
rising over the rounded bluffs, and throwing his
beams obliquely along the surface of the turbid
Missouri. The prairie was clad in its richest
apparel. The young grass covered it with a
thick sward, which still preserved the living
freshness and beautiful verdure of spring, and
flowers, infinite in number, as diversified in hue,
reared their heads to the surface of the grassy
carpet, and seemed to repose upon it, like colours
upon the canvass of the painter. The whole plain
presented a series of graceful swells and depres-
sions, which, at this early hour of the day, received the sunlight under such a variety of angles,
as to afford an endless diversity of light and shade;
while it heightened the effect of the perspective,
by throwing up a few points into prominent relief,
and casting others, whose features were as distinctly visible, into an imaginary back-ground.

As the cavalcade commenced its march, a long
train of warriors, on horseback, were beheld issuing from the village, arrayed in all the pomp, and
in all the grave dignity, of Indian display. Their
faces were carefully painted in the best style,
some gaily, with a profusion of crimson, others
lowering in the gloomy ferocity of black, while
their bodies were adorned with the trapping of
savage magnificence, and their heads arrayed in
feathers of a variety of gaudy hues. They were
armed with the numerous implements of war and
hunting—with guns, bows, war-clubs, tomahawks,
and knives—and mounted upon small active horses,
with vicious eyes and untamed spirits, that evinced
submission to the power of their riders, but not
affection for their persons. Some rode without
stirrups, some on saddles richly ornamented. The
bridles of many were decorated with gaudy coloured ribbon, tape, or tinsel, or with bits of tin,
or pieces of dressed deer skin cut into fringe, or
rolled into tassels; and many had adorned the
manes and tails of their horses. Although, in the
appearance of some of these native warriors, the
grotesque predominated, while extreme poverty
was displayed in the equipment of others, there
was observable in each, the same unconstrained
air, and indescribable wildness, peculiar to this
original people; and there were a few warriors
mounted on fine horses, well clad, completely

armed and appointed, of sedate carriage, and
military bearing, and whose whole conduct bore
the decisive stamp of dignity. They moved
slowly; but here and there might be seen a young
brave urging his horse rapidly along the flank of
the column, or seeking to attract attention by
dashing off from the party, across the plain, at full
speed, with his feet pressed in his courser's sides,
his body bent forward, his buffalo spear poised, as
if for striking, and his long plume of feathers
streaming upon the wind. Behind the main body
of horsemen, followed the squaws, the children,
and the old men, a few of whom were mounted on
lean ponies, but the greater part on foot, trudging
soberly along—except the younger females, who
amused themselves with jeering any of the junior
warriors who happened to lag behind their comrades. Under charge of this body of non-combat-
ants, was a train of pack-horses, bearing the mats,
skin lodges, and other moveables. On the packs
might be seen many a little urchin, too big to be
carried on his mother's back, yet too small to
walk, who enjoyed the high privilege of being
lashed to the baggage, and treated as an article
of furniture—where he sat comfortably enough,
poking out his dark face from among the pack-
ages, and staring with his little wild black eyes,
like a copper-headed snake. With this part of
the cavalcade, too, were the dogs, who, when not

abroad on duty with their masters, usually seek the society of the ladies, and the agreeable atmosphere of the culinary department. Those in question were particularly given to these lounging habits, and for ever stealing after the flesh pots, and endeavouring to curry favour with the women. From their appearance, one would suppose their company not to have been desirable; for the Indian's dog is a lean, hungry, ferocious animal, who gets more kicks than favours, and who sneaks about, with his bushy tail drooped, his pointed ears erect, his long nose thrust forward, and his watchful eye gleaming with mischief and distrust. Resembling the wolf in appearance and manners, he seems to be obedient from fear only, and to have little in common with the generous and affectionate animal, who is the friend, as well as the servant, of civilised man, and of whom the poet testified, when he said, " they are *honest* creatures."

On leaving the village, the Indian train ascended a long gradual swell, until they reached a beautifully rounded eminence, that commanded an extensive view of the prairie, over which they were about to travel. Nothing could be more striking than this wild picture of native luxuriance, and aboriginal pomp. A wide expanse of scenery was spread before the eye. The interminable plain seemed to extend further than the vision could

reach ; and there was something peculiarly picturesque in the march of the Omawhaws, whose
long party-coloured line wound and undulated
among the slopes and mounds of the prairie,
headed by armed warriors, and flanked by young
horsemen, darting off from the main body to show
the speed of their horses, and displaying their own
dexterity by a variety of evolutions.

When the party reached the most elevated point
of the plain, it halted, and a glance was thrown
back towards the deserted wigwams. Not a living
thing moved in the village, whose lowly huts, un-
tenanted and still, seemed to form a part of the
natural landscape. Beyond it flowed the broad
and turbulent Missouri, and further towards the
east, was a range of low, pointed hills, whose
sides were thinly clothed with timber, while their
bald summits were covered with only a verdant
carpet of grass. The newly risen sun had just
appeared beyond these hills, lighting up their
peaked tops with the full effulgence of his splendour, and strongly marking the characteristic
horizon of this peculiar region of country. Over
this scene they gazed for a few moments with
comtion, for some of them might never return to
the wigwams of their tribe, and those who should
survive might find their fields ravaged, and the
graves of their fathers desecrated. Even an Indian loves his home. Erratic as are his habits,

and little as he seems to understand or enjoy domestic comfort, he acquires, unconsciously, an attachment towards the spot on which he resides, and a reverence for the associations by which it is surrounded. There are dear and joyful recollections connected with the fireside, however humble it may be; and the turf that covers the remains of departed friends, is as holy in the eyes of the uneducated savage, who has never been taught to analyse the operations of his own mind, as in those of the person of refinement, who recognises the good taste and virtuous feeling of this natural emotion of the heart.

Bolingbroke was not the man to appreciate an interesting landscape, or to sympathise with a flow of tender feeling. He sat on his horse, apart from the others, and was calculating the probable advantages of an union with the daughter of the chief of the Omawhaws, and revolving in his mind the means by which he might most speedily bring about so desirable an alliance, when the Blackbird himself rode up beside him.

"Is the *Wise Stranger* sorrowful in spirit," said the chief, "or does he regret that the Omawhaws are quitting the graves of their fathers?"

"Neither," replied Bolingbroke; "the Great Spirit has not thrown any cloud over the heart of his white son, and the graves that we are leaving are not those of *my* fathers."

"Then why should the trader of the white people be sad, when his red brethren are going to hunt on the plains where the buffaloes feed?"

"I am thinking of something that I had forgotten."

"Has the Master of life told my friend in a dream, that he has failed to do something which he ought to have done?"

"Yes, my father; even thus has the Master of life whispered to my heart, while my eyes were sleeping. I have seen my fault. But I feel comforted by the reflection that the great chief of the Omawhaws is my friend."

The chief directed a calm though penetrating glance of enquiry towards his companion, but the countenance of the trader betrayed no emotion. It was evident the offence was not one of deep dye. His eye wandered back to the cavalcade, and rested proudly on the warrior train. The young trader resumed:

"My father has always been kind to the white stranger."

"The pale face has reason to believe that the Blackbird is his friend," replied the chief.

"I have endeavoured to convince the great chief that I desire to serve him. I have no other pleasure than to make the Omawhaws happy, by supplying their wants."

21

"The white man has done his duty—I am satisfied."

Here a pause ensued, and these well-matched politicians gazed along the line, which was now beginning to be again set in motion—each endeavouring stealthily to catch a glance at the countenance of the other. The young merchant was the first to renew the conversation.

"In making my presents to the chiefs," he said, "I endeavoured to distinguish those who were most worthy, and who stood highest in the estimation of the Omawhaws, by the value of the gifts which I made them. But I fear that I did not sufficiently recollect the high claims of the Blackbird, who is elevated above all others by his wisdom, his many victories, and his friendship for the white people. I am a young man, and the Great Spirit has not been pleased to give me that wisdom which he reserves for great chiefs, whose business is to govern tribes."·

As he said this, he drew from his bosom an elegantly mounted dirk, a favourite ornament and weapon of the Indian.

"Will the head man of the Omawhaws," continued he, presenting it, "accept this as a small part of the atonement which my negligence imposes on me; and depend upon my word, that, in future, I shall not forget the distance between a great chief and his inferiors?"

"The white stranger has been very properly called *wise*," said the chief, "and the head man of the Omawhaws knows how to value his friends. I have looked back at our path ;—it is all white— there is no cloud there. The white trader may know hereafter that the Blackbird is his friend."

Thus saying, he eyed the beautiful weapon which he had received with complacency, drew it, and examined the blade—passing his eye along it with the keen scrutiny of one intimately versed in the mechanism and use of military implements ; then, having arranged it in the most conspicuous manner upon his person, he rode away, muttering to himself, "What does the trader want in return for so fine a present?" He did not dream that Bolingbroke wanted his daughter.

In a few days they arrived at the pastures of the buffalo, and beheld the plains covered with herds of wild cattle. The animating scenes of the hunt commenced. Parties of hunters, mounted upon fleet horses well trained to this sport, dashed in among the grazing herds. At their approach the buffaloes fled in alarm ; the hunters pursued at full speed, each horseman selecting his victim. The swiftness of the horse soon outstripped the speed of the buffalo, and placed the hunter by the side of his noble game ; when, dropping the bridle, while his trained steed continued to bear him gallantly along, side by side, with the buffalo, he discharged his arrows into the panting animal, until it fell mortally wounded. Then the hunter, quitting his prey, dashed again into the affrighted herd to select another.

It was an inspiring sight to behold the wide plain,—an immense meadow, studded with ornamental groves,—covered with numerous herds, quietly grazing like droves of domestic cattle : then to see the Omawhaw bands, under the cover of some copse or swelling ground, covertly approaching from the leeward, so that the timid animals might not scent their approach in the tainted breeze ; and, at last, to view the confusion occasioned by their sudden onset. On discovering their enemies, the alarmed herd, following its leaders, would attempt to move away rapidly in a solid phalanx ; but the hunters, penetrating boldly into the heart of the retreating body, dispersed it in every direction—and the maddened animals were seen flying towards all points of the compass, followed by the fierce wild hunters. The vicissitudes of the chase were numerous and diversified. Sometimes a horse fell, and the prostrate rider was saluted with loud shouts of derision ; sometimes a large bull turned suddenly upon his pursuer, and burying his horns deep in the flanks of the steed, hurled him upon the plain ; and more than once the hunter, thus thrown, with difficulty escaped being trodden to death by the furious herd.

Bolingbroke engaged with ardour in this sport.
He was a skilful and daring horseman; and though
at first awkward, from his ignorance of the artifices
of the chase, he soon became sufficiently expert to
be considered as an useful auxiliary by his companions. The warriors began to treat him with
increased respect; and even the squaws, whose
favour he had heretofore conciliated by timely
presents, looked upon him with more complacency, after witnessing these displays of his activity
and courage.

A daring horseman gallops rapidly into a lady's
affections. The sex admire intrepidity, and give
their suffrages decidedly in favour of a dashing
fellow who combines boldness with grace and
skill. Bolingbroke found favour in the eyes of
the New Moon; and, though she carefully concealed her sentiments in her own bosom, he soon
ceased to be an object of indifference. He was
her father's friend, and she began to discover that
it was her duty to admire his exploits and approve
his conduct. One day, as he was returning to
camp alone from a successful hunt, he overtook
the fair Menac, who was also separated accidentally from the company. It was an opportunity too
favourable to be lost. As he joined her she threw
her eyes upon the ground, and walked silently forward. He dismounted, and throwing his bridle

21*

over his arm, placed himself at the side of the Omawhaw beauty.

How awkward it is to begin a conversation under such circumstances! Among us, a remark on the weather would have furnished a theme for the lovers to begin upon; but these meteorological discussions were not fashionable at the Omawhaw village. One of Miss Edgeworth's heroes pulled a flower to pieces, on a similar occasion, before he could open his mouth; but Bolingbroke was a man of business, and came at once to the point.

"The daughter of Blackbird looks upon the ground," said he; "she does not seem pleased to see the white friend of her father."

"The white stranger is glad because he has had a good hunt," replied the maiden, "and others seem to him to be sad, because they are not so joyful as himself."

"When I look at the New Moon," rejoined the lover, "my heart is always filled with gladness, for she is very beautiful."

"I have often heard," replied Menae, "that the white men have forked tongues, and do not mean what they say."

"Others may have lying lips, but mine are true. I have never deceived the Omawhaws. I speak truth, when I say that I love the beautiful Menae, for she is handsomer than all the other daughters of her tribe. If she will be my wife, I

will build a wigwam in the village of the Omawhaws, and quit for ever the graves of my fathers,
and the council fires of the white people."

"The wise stranger would send a cloud over
his father's house. How many of the girls of the
pale faces are looking up the great river, to see
him return, as he promised them?" enquired she,
archly.

"Not one! not one! You are the only woman
I have ever loved—I will never love another.
Become my wife, and I promise you, here in
the presence of the Master of life, that I will never
seek the love of any other. Menae shall be the
sole companion, and dearest friend, of my life."

"I am the daughter of a great chief," replied
the Indian maid.

"Ah! I understand you—you are too proud to
marry one who is not of your nation."

"The roaring of the buffalo has made the ear
of the white hunter dull. I am the daughter of a
chief, and I may not give myself away."

"Lovely Menae!" exclaimed the youth, as he
attempted to seize her hand; but she quietly
folded her arms, and looked at him with composure, assuming a dignity which effectually repelled
any further advance. She then addressed him
with a touching softness of voice.

"There is a path to my heart which is right;
it is a straight path." She paused; but her eye,

which beamed softly upon her lover, expressed all that he could have wished. She added, "If the white trader is wise, as men say he is, he will not attempt to gain a young maiden's affections by any crooked way."

So saying, she walked quietly away, while the politic trader, who understood her meaning, respectfully withdrew, satisfied that the lady would interpose no objection to his suit, if the consent of a higher authority could be secured.

Having taken his resolution, he proceeded to the lodge of the Blackbird, and endeavoured to conciliate the favour of both the parents of Menac by liberal presents. He adverted artfully to the advantages which would accrue to both parties by an alliance between the chief and himself, avowed his love for their daughter, and his decided wish to marry one of the Omawhaw tribe. He promised, if they would transfer their daughter to him in marriage, to treat her kindly, and to introduce no other wife into his lodge. He suggested that he had now established a permanent trading house at their village, where he should reside during the greater part of the year, and where he would be fully able to protect and support, both his proposed wife, and her kindred, if necessary. In return, he hoped the nation would give him the preference in their trade, and consider him as one allied to them in affection and interest.

To this very business like harangue, which was sufficiently sentimental for the ears to which it was addressed, the parents made a suitable reply. They thanked him for his liberal offers, and were gratified that he had taken pity on their daughter; they would not object to the connection, and hoped their daughter would accept him. The mother added that Menae was stronger than she looked, and could carry a great many skins; and, though she was not very expert in tending corn, she was young enough to learn. The chief gave him the comfortable assurance that it was quite indifferent to them how many wives he might choose to have, provided he could support and govern them—for his part, he had had his own trouble with one; but he commended the prudence of his young friend in confining himself to a single squaw for the present, until he should become experienced in the inequalities of the female temper, and have learned the difficult art of ruling a household.

The parents retired, and opened the subject to their daughter, to whom they magnified the advantages of the proposed alliance, with one who was, in their opinion, a greater man than any of the Omawhaws. His wealth exceeded that of all the tribe; his store of guns, ammunition, trinkets, and clothing, seemed to be inexhaustible; and they earnestly requested her to secure her own happiness, and advance the interests of her family, by accepting an offer so tempting.

The *New Moon*, though delighted with her conquest, thought it proper, as young ladies are apt to think, on such occasions, to support her dignity by affecting some reluctance. In the first place, the gentleman's complexion was against him, and she would have given any thing—except himself—if it had been a shade or two darker. Then his taste in dress was by no means such as accorded with her ideas of manly beauty ; and she regretted that he did not paint his handsome face, decorate his hair with the feathers of the eagle, ornament his nasal protuberance with rings, and cover his shoulders with the ample folds of a Makinaw blanket. Above all, he had never struck an enemy in battle ; not a single scalp attested his prowess as a warrior ; and although he managed a horse with skill, and had wielded the rifle successfully in the chase, he was as ignorant as a woman of the use of a tomahawk, or a scalping knife. Notwithstanding all this, she admitted that the white trader was wise—he was young, had a good eye, and a stout arm, and might, in time, with proper tuition, become worthy to be ranked among the head men of the Omawhaws. Upon the whole, she expressed her own unworthiness, her ignorance of what would be right on such an occasion, her willingness to obey the wishes of her parents, and to advance the interests of her nation ; and as it seemed to be their desire, and her duty, she would marry the trader.

They were united accordingly, and the beautiful Menae entered upon a new existence. Marriage always affects a decided change upon the sentiments of those, who come within its sacred pale under a proper sense of the responsibilities of the married state. However delightful the intercourse of wedded hearts, there is, to a well-regulated mind, something extremely solemn in the duties imposed by this interesting relation. The reflection that an existence which was separate and independent is ended, and that all its hopes and interests are blended with those of another soul, is deeply affecting, as it imposes the conviction that every act which shall influence the happiness of the one, will colour the destiny of the other. But when the union is that of love, this feeling of dependence is one of the most delightful that can be imagined. It annihilates the habit of selfish enjoyment, and teaches the heart to delight in that which gives pleasure to another. The affections become gradually enlarged, expanding as the ties of relationship, and the duties of life accumulate around, until the individual, ceasing to know an isolated existence, lives entirely for others, and for society.

But it is the generous and the virtuous alone,

who thus enjoy this agreeable relation. Some
hearts there are, too callous to give nurture to a
delicate sentiment. There are minds too narrow
to give play to an expansive benevolence. A certain degree of magnanimity is necessary to the
existence of disinterested love, or friendship.

The beautiful Menae was of a noble generous
nature. She had never been selfish, and now that
her affections had an object on which to concen-
trate their warmth, her heart glowed with disinterested emotion. With a native ingenuousness
of soul, that had always induced her, even without
reflection, to consult the happiness of others in
preference to her own, she had now an object
whose interests were so dear, that it was as delightful, as it was natural, to sacrifice to them all
her own inclinations. From the moment of her
marriage, she began to adapt her conduct to the
taste of her husband. She adopted his opinions,
imitated his manners, and gradually exchanged
the ornaments of her tribe for those which accorded better with his fancy. It cost her not a pang,
nor a regret, to throw aside the costume which
she had considered graceful, and had worn with
pride in the meridian of her beauty, and to invest
her charms in a foreign drapery, which was far
less becoming in her own eyes. Whatever her
husband admired, became graceful in her estimation; and that which rendered her attractive to

him, she wore with more than youthful delight.
A similar change took place in her domestic
arrangements. Instead of the rude wigwam of
the Indian, Bolingbroke had built a small but
neat cottage, and had furnished it with some of
the comforts, though few of the luxuries, of his
country, and his wife eagerly endeavoured to
gratify his wishes, by adapting herself to his
habits of living. She learned to sit upon a chair,
to eat from a table, and to treat her husband as a
companion rather than as a master. Hour after
hour did she listen attentively to his descriptions of
the habits of his countrywomen, and carefully did
she treasure up in her memory every hint which
might serve as a guide in her endeavour to render
her own deportment pleasing to him to whom she
had given an unreserved affection. From him
she had learned to attach a name, and an endear-
ing value, to the spot which he called his *home ;*
and, for his sake, she sought to throw every en-
chantment around the scene of their domestic
enjoyments. With all that wonderful facility with
which the female heart, when stimulated by the
desire of pleasing, can mould itself to the wishes of
another, she caught his opinions, and learned to
understand his tastes—entwining her own existence around his, as the ivy clings to the oak.
Her cottage soon became conspicuous for its neatness and beauty. She transplanted the wild rose

and the honeysuckle, from the woods, and trained
them over her door, in imitation of the bowers
that he had described to her.   Her table was
spread with the dainties which he had taught her
to prepare, her furniture arranged in the order
which he dictated, and all her household duties
directed with the nicest regard to his feelings or
prejudices.

And had she no prejudices to be respected—no
habits to be indulged—no wishes to be gratified?
None.   She loved with the pure devotion of a
generous woman.   She had a heart which could
sacrifice every selfish wish upon the altar of affection—a mind so resolute in the performance of
duty, that it could magnanimously stifle every
desire that ran counter to its own high standard
of rectitude.   She possessed talent and feeling—
and to those ideas of implicit obedience, and profound respect for her husband, which constitute
nearly the whole code of ethics of an Indian female, she added a nice perception of propriety,
and a tenderness that filled her whole heart.   She
had no reserved rights.   She was too generous to
give a divided affection.   In giving herself to her
husband she severed all other ties, and merged
her whole existence in his—and the language of
her heart was, "thy people shall be my people,
and thy God my God."   Such is the hallowed
principle of woman's love—such the pure senti-

ment, the deep devotion, the high-minded elevation
of that passion, when sanctioned by duty, in the
bosom of a well-principled and delicate female!

The New Moon of the Omawhaws was a proud
and happy wife. Her young affections reposed
sweetly in the luxury of a blameless attachment.
She had married the man of her choice, who had
freely selected her from all her tribe. That man
was greater than those around him, and, in her
eyes, superior to most of his sex. He had distinguished and honoured her. He had taken her to
his bosom, given her his confidence, surrounded
her with luxuries and marks of kindness.

Yet there were some thorns in her path; and,
in the midst of all the brightness of her sunniest
days, her dream of bliss was sometimes chilled by
clouds that threw their dim shadows over it. Almost unconsciously to herself a sadness would rest
for a moment upon her heart, and fly before she
had time to enquire whence it came. There was
a dark spot in her destiny, of the existence of
which she was scarcely sensible, because she
turned her eyes away from it in fear or in pride.
A chill sometimes crept over her heart, but, without waiting to enquire into its cause, she chased it
away, gazed again upon the bright vision of her
wedded joy, and forgot that an unpleasant image
had been present. Was it the occasional coldness
of Bolingbroke, who, immersed in the cares of

business, or abstracted in the anticipations of a future affluence, received the endearments of his wife with indifference? Or was it the estranged deportment of her tribe, who began to regard her as an alien? She knew not—she never permitted herself to doubt the love of her husband, and she prized the affection of others too little, to enquire into the ebb and flow of its tide.

The time, however, arrived when Menac began to discover that she had a difficult task to perform. Her husband was a trader, bent on the accumulation of wealth by catching every gale of fortune that might chance to blow—her relatives, and those by whom she was surrounded, were fierce and crafty savages, ignorant of the principles of justice, and destitute of any fixed standard of moral right. His interests and theirs were often opposed; and while he was always prepared to reap the spoil of their labours, they were as ready to crush or to plunder him whenever he happened to cross their purposes, or to awaken their suspicion. His popularity rose and fell with the changes of the season. A new supply of goods rendered him the idol of the tribe—an exhausted stock exposed him to insult and injustice. Previous to the annual hunt, or to a warlike expedition, he was flattered and obeyed by those improvident warriors, who, having made no preparations for such an occasion, were dependent upon him for the outfit which was necessary to enable them to take the field; but when the spoils of the chase or of battle came to be divided, and the largest portion was claimed by the trader in payment of his debts, he became for the moment an object of hatred—and it required all the power of the chiefs, and all the cunning of his own politic brain, to secure him from their vengeance. On such occasions he found his wife an invaluable counsellor, and an efficient friend. Her influence with the tribe was by no means contemptible. Her own popularity, and her ready access to the ear of her father, whom all others feared to approach, gave her a degree of authority among the warriors, which she seldom used, and never exerted in vain.

But her influence was gradually diminishing. As Bolingbroke grew rich he became more and more rapacious. The other traders were practising every popular art to recommend themselves, to destroy him, and to rise upon the ruins of his prosperity; and his vigilant wife had more than once protected his life and property, by discovering the designs of his enemies, and secretly appealing to her father for protection. These things, however, did not disturb her peace. Vigilant by nature—accustomed to danger from childhood, and inured to all the vicissitudes of the savage mode of life—she could watch with composure over a husband's safety, and expose her own exist-

22*

ence without fear. Perhaps, to one of her habits, the excitement of such a life was agreeable; and she certainly felt a pride in becoming thus important to him who was the sole object of her love.

But while she despised the machinations of her husband's foes, with all the disdain of a proud woman, it was not without uneasiness that she discovered a sensible diminution in the cordiality of her own friends. She had married one who was an alien to her tribe, and such marriages always produce estrangement. They saw her abandoning the customs of her country, and throwing aside the dress of her people. She mingled but little with the women of the Omawhaws; and while she tacitly condemned some of their practices by her own deportment, she withdrew her sanction from some of their ancient rites by her absence. Her improvements in domestic economy were regarded with ridicule and jealousy. The young warriors no longer regarded her with pride as the beauty of their nation, but considered her as one who had apostatised from the customs of her fathers, and degraded herself by linking her destiny with that of a stranger from a foreign land. She felt that she, who had been the idol of the tribe, was sustained by the wealth of her husband and the power of her father, and not by the affection of those around her.

It was the custom of Bolingbroke to descend

the river annually to St. Louis, for the purpose of
renewing his stock of merchandise—and he had
been married but a few months when the first
absence of this kind occurred. On his return, his
young wife received him with the utmost tenderness. He was charmed to hear of the discretion
with which she had conducted herself in his absence, and to perceive the many evidences of the
manner in which she had spent her time. He
learned that she had lived a retired life, engaging
in none of the public festivals, and receiving few
visiters at her house. She had laboured inces-
santly in decorating their dwelling, or in fabricat-
ing such articles of dress for her husband as she
thought would please his fancy; while she had
noticed with careful attention the movements of
the tribe, and gathered up every rumour, the
intelligence of which might be useful to him in
his mercantile concerns.

Another year came, and again he left her. His
absence was protracted during several months,
and within this period she became the mother
of a daughter, which she nursed with the fondest
solicitude. Her love for her husband, and her
anxiety for his return, seemed to increase after
this event. With her infant in her arms, she
wandered out daily to a secluded spot on the bank
of the river, where she would sit for hours, following the downward course of the river with

eager eyes to gain the earliest notice of his approach. Estimating his feelings by her own, she was impatient for the moment when she could place the interesting stranger in his arms, and see him gaze with delight at that beautiful miniature in which each might see the features of the other. Nor was she disappointed. Bolingbroke caressed his child with fondness, and she was the happiest of mothers—the proudest of wives.

We must touch briefly upon the subsequent events of this narrative. Another and another year rolled away, and Menac was still the devoted wife, while Bolingbroke was become a cold, though a civil, husband : he bending all his energies to the acquisition of wealth, she bringing in her diurnal tribute of love, and living only to promote his happiness. They had now two children, and when the time approached for his annual visit to the settlements of the white people, he proposed to carry the eldest with him. The wife, always obedient, reluctantly consented, and commanded her feelings so far, as to behold their departure in mute, suppressed affliction. But, although one charge remained, upon which she might lavish her caresses, no sooner had her husband commenced his voyage, than her maternal fondness overpowered her, and she ran screaming along the shore of the river, in pursuit of the boat, tearing out her long glossy tresses, and appearing almost bereft of reason. Unable to overtake the boat, she returned disconsolate, and assumed the deepest mourning which the customs of her tribe impose on the state of widowhood. She cut off her beautiful raven locks, gave away her ornaments, and every thing that she had worn in her day of pride, and clothed herself in humble attire. Confining herself to her own dwelling, she refused the visits of her friends, and repelled their offers of consolation. She said that she well knew that her daughter would be better treated among the whites, than she could be at home, but she could not avoid regarding her own situation to be the same as if the Wahcondah had taken away her offspring for ever.

By degrees her remaining child began to absorb the entire current of her affections, and, on his account, she resumed the performance of her household duties, though she would not throw aside her mourning. One day, she had gone in company with some other females to the corn-fields, adjoining the village, and was engaged in agricultural labours, her infant boy being secured, after the Indian fashion, to a board, which she had carefully leaned against a tree. They were discovered by a lurking war-party of Sioux, who rushed upon them suddenly, in the expectation of gratifying their vengeance by the massacre of the whole party. An exclamation of terror, uttered by one of the

females, on discovering the enemy, caused the
alarmed women to fly precipitately ; and Menae,
in the first moment of affright, was in the act of
retreating with the others, when she recollected
her child. To save a life more precious than her
own, she swiftly returned, in the face of the Sioux
warriors, snatched her child from the tree, and
bore him rapidly away. She was closely pursued
by one of the savages, who had nearly overtaken
her, when she arrived at a fence which separated
the field from the enclosure surrounding the trading-house. A moment's hesitation would have
been fatal—but, with a presence of mind which
always distinguished her above other women, she
gathered all her strength, threw the child, with
its board, into the enclosure, and then, placing her
hands on the fence, leaped nimbly over. Several
of her companions were murdered, while she
escaped, with her child, unhurt.*

After a longer absence than usual, Bolingbroke
returned, bringing with him an accomplished lady,
of his own people, whom he had married, but un-
accompanied by his Indian daughter, whom he
had placed at school. Menae heard this intelligence with the deepest sorrow, but with less surprise than such an event would have occasioned a

* I am indebted to Long's Expedition for this, and some
of the other incidents of this tale.

wife in a civilised land; as the practice of poly-
gamy, which prevails among the Omawhaws, had
perhaps prepared her to anticipate such an occur-
ence as not improbable. She was stung to the
heart by the conviction that she had lost the love
of him, who was dearer to her than all the world,
and for whom she had sacrificed so much; and
mortified that another should be preferred to herself. But the legality of the transaction, and its
frequency among the people of her tribe, lulled, in
some degree, the sense of degradation, and blunted
the sharpness of her resentment. She considered
the act lawful, while she condemned the actor as
faithless and ungrateful. In secresy she wept
bitterly over her disappointed pride, and blighted
joy; but professed in public a cheerful acquiescence in the decision of her husband. The Blackbird was now dead; and the keen sighted Menac
could not blind herself to the conviction, that the
decease of her father had rendered her of less importance to the mercenary trader.

Previous to the arrival of Bolingbroke at the
Omawhaw village, he despatched a message to
the trading-house, announcing his marriage, and
forbidding his Indian wife from appearing in the
presence of her rival. To this cruel mandate she
submitted, with that implicit obedience which the
females of her race are accustomed to pay to the
commands of their husbands, and departed to a

distant village of her nation. But what woman
can trust the weakness of her heart? Conjugal
love, and maternal fondness, both allured her to
the presence of him who had so long been the
master of her affections. Which of these was the
prevailing inducement, it is difficult to conjecture ;
she longed to see Bolingbroke, and her heart
yearned for tidings from her absent child, but
without this plea, her pride would probably have
forbidden her from seeking an interview with the
destroyer of her peace. Unable to remain in
banishment, she returned to her native village,
with her little boy on her back, and encamped in
the neighbourhood of her husband's residence—in
sight of that cottage which her own hands had
embellished, in which she had spent years of domestic felicity, and where another now reigned in
her place. She sent her son to the trader, who
treated him affectionately. On the following day
he commanded her presence, and she stood before
him, in that house which had been her own, with
her arms meekly folded upon her breast, gazing
calmly on the cold but handsome features of him
who was the lord of her destiny. Suppressing
every other feeling, and avoiding all other topics,
she enquired for her daughter, and listened with
interest to such information as he was pleased to
give her. She then, with much composure, desired to know his intentions in relation to the

future disposition of both her children. To this question he gave an evasive answer; and directed her to accompany her friends, who were on their way to the hunting grounds. She departed without a murmur.

•Two months afterwards, she was recalled. She lost no time in presenting herself before the husband whom she still tenderly loved, notwithstanding his cruel desertion. Her resentment had in a great measure subsided, and rather than be banished entirely from his affection, she was content to share it with another, according to the usages of her tribe. Such she supposed to be his intention in sending for her, and she freely forgave the temporary aberration of his love, under the supposition that she would be to him hereafter, if not his sole favourite, at least a respected wife, that her children would find a home under his roof, and that he would be to her, and them, a faithful protector. Alas! how the heart, given up to the illusions of love, cheats itself with visions of future bliss! How often does the young wife build up a fabric of happiness, which, like the icy palace of the Russian potentate, is splendid to the eye in the hour of its illumination, but melts away with the sun of the succeeding day! The New Moon hastened to her husband, full of young hope, and newly kindled affection; but bitter was her disappointment, when, after an austere reception, he

23

demanded the surrender of her son, and renounced
any future association with herself, directing her
to return to her people, and to provide for her own
support as she might see proper.

Indignant at being thus repudiated, overcome
by feelings which she could not control, and
alarmed at the proposed separation from her
child, she rushed from the house with the infant
in her arms, and finding a canoe on the river
shore, paddled over to the opposite side, and made
her escape into the forest. The weather was
cold and stormy, the snow was falling, and the
wretched mother had no shelter to protect her.
Throughout the whole night she wandered about
in the wilderness, hugging her babe to her bosom,
and keeping it alive by the warmth of her own
breast. But worn down with fatigue and exposure,
and discouraged by her disconsolate condition, she
determined in the morning to return, and, with the
feelings of a wife and mother, to plead her cause
before the arbiter of her fate.

Early in the morning, the wretched woman,
faint, hungry, and shivering with cold, presented
herself before him, who, in the hour of her beauty,
had sued for her favour. She, who had loved,
and cherished, and counselled, and protected him,
and who had higher claims upon him than any
other living individual, stood a trembling suppliant
at his door.

"Here is our child," said she ; "I do not question your fondness for him—but he is still more dear to me. You can not love him with a mother's love, nor keep him with a mother's care. You say that you will keep him for yourself, and drive me far from you. But, no—I will remain with him. You may spurn me from your own society, but you cannot drive me from my child. Take him and feed him. I can find some corner into which I may creep, in order to be near him, and hear him when he cries for his mother, and sometimes see him. If you will not give me food, I will remain until I starve, and die before your eyes."

There are those who have no feeling. The trader had none. Not a chord in his bosom vibrated to this eloquent appeal. A young and beautiful woman reduced to penury—a mother folding her infant in her arms—his own wife, the mother of his children—she who had cherished his interest and honour more dearly than her own life, and who would have endured any anguish to have saved him from a momentary pang ;—with all these, and a thousand other claims upon his sympathy and justice, she was an unsuccessful suppliant.

He offered her money, and desired her to leave the child. Her blood rushed to her heart at the base proposal, and she indignantly replied—"Is

my child a dog, that I should sell him for merchandise? You cannot drive me away; you may
beat me, you may taunt me with insults, but I will
remain. When you married me, you promised to
use me kindly as long as I should be faithful to
you; that I have always been so, no one can deny.
I have loved you with tenderness, and served you
with fidelity. Ours was not a marriage contracted
for a season—it was to terminate only with our
lives. I was then a young girl, the daughter of
the head man of the Omawhaws, and might have
been united to a chief of my own nation; but now
I am an old woman, the mother of two children,
and what Omawhaw will regard me? Is not my
right superior to that of your other wife? She
had heard of me before you possessed her. It is
true, her skin is whiter than mine, but her heart
cannot be more pure towards you, nor her fidelity
more rigid. Do not take the child from my breast
—I cannot bear to hear it cry, and not be present
to relieve it: permit me to retain it until the
spring, when it will be able to eat, and then, if it
must be so, take it from my sight, that I may part
with it but once."

The trader remained inexorable; he listened,
with apathy, to the feeling appeal of his wife; but
finding her inflexible, and knowing her high spirit,
he attempted no reply—coolly remarking that she
might remain there if she pleased, but that the

child should immediately be sent down to the settlements.

The affectionate mother had thus far sustained herself, during the interview, with the firmness of conscious right, and had successfully curbed the impulse of her feelings; but nature now yielded, the tears burst from her eyes—and clasping her hands, and bowing her head, she gave way to the agony of her grief, exclaiming—" Why did the Master of life hate me so much, as to induce me to put my child again into your power?"

" But, no," she continued, after a momentary pause, " we are not in your power—you have renounced my obedience—I no longer owe you any duty. I belong to a free wild race that has never submitted to oppression. The pale face shall learn that the blood of an Omawhaw chief runs in the veins of his discarded wife. For herself, she has no wrongs to resent—but for her child she can strike the death-blow with as firm an arm as that of the warrior. My son shall not go to the fires of the white people, to be their servant, and to be insulted for his descent from an Indian mother. He shall not be trained up in the corn-field like a squaw, or be taught to sell his honour for money like the trader of the white Americans. I shall take him with me. He is mine, and shall never be taken alive from my arms. Attempt to separate us, and I will strike this knife to his heart,

23*

and then put an end to my own wretched existence!"

So saying, she darted away with a swiftness
which announced that the resolution of her mind
had imparted new vigour to her limbs; while the
trader, alarmed by her threats, abandoned his purpose, and suffered her to retire without pursuit.

Two weeks afterwards, a haggard female was
seen slowly approaching a distant hunting-camp
of the Omawhaws, bearing an emaciated child on
her back. It was she who had once been the
pride of their nation—the daughter of that dreaded
chief whose word was law. She had wandered
through the woods, thinly clad, and almost without
food, subsisting upon such small game as she could
entrap by artifice. At night she crept into a hollow tree, or scraped the snow from the ground,
and nestled in the leaves. She had traversed the
wide prairies, now desolate and snow clad, on whose
broad expanse scarce a living animal was seen, and
over which the bleak wind swept with unbroken
power. The wolf had tracked her footsteps, and
howled around the dreary spot of her lonesome
encampment. Without a path or a guide—ignorant of the intended movements of her tribe, and
uncertain where to find them—exposed to immi-
nent and constantly impending danger from cold,
hunger, beasts of prey, and hostile savages—this
intrepid female pursued her solitary way through

the vast wilderness with unbroken spirit, trusting
to her native courage and sagacity, and praying to
the Great Master of life for assistance. And who
doubts that such a prayer is heard? Who can
doubt that the same beneficent God who decks the
wilderness with matchless beauty, and stores it
with abundance, listens to the plaintive cry of the
widowed mother and her innocent babe? How
often do the weak and helpless pass unhurt through
perils under which the bold and strong would sink,
or endure privations for the support of which humanity seems unequal! And can we see this without believing that the same unseen influence, which
tempers the wind to the shorn lamb, is ever ready
to listen to the petition of the afflicted?—and that
those who seem most friendless and destitute are
the favoured objects of the most efficient protection? Yes—there is a prayer that is heard,
though it ascend not from the splendid edifices
erected by pride or piety, nor clothes itself in the
rounded periods of polished eloquence. There is
a religion of the heart, and a language of nature;
and God, who so organised the flower that it turns
itself to the sun, to catch vigour from the life-giv-
ing ray, has so framed the human bosom that it
spontaneously expands itself to Him in the hour of
adversity. She prayed to the Great Spirit, and
he conducted her safely through the wilderness.

The Omawhaws had regarded the wife of Bo-

lingbroke with coldness, when they saw her surrounded with affluence superior to their own, and
considered her as an apostate from the ancient
customs of her people. Their love for her was
turned to distrust, while they beheld her in a
foreign garb, and viewed her as the ally of the
white man. But when she came back to them a
destitute, houseless, deserted woman, they received
her with kindness, restored her to the place she
had occupied in their confidence, and poured out
bitter curses upon her faithless husband. As she
repeated the story of her abandonment, even in
the softened language of an unwilling accuser,
their indignant comments showed that they had
made her cause their own. Bolingbroke was no
longer protected by the mysterious power of the
dreaded chief, his rivals had already supplanted
him in the affections of the tribe, and his last
offence overturned the tottering fabric of his popularity. The passions of the Indian know no
medium : what they condemn they hate, and whatever they hate they destroy. The doom of the
trader was deliberately fixed. It was unsparing
and irrevocable. Him, and his household, and all
that he possessed, were solemnly doomed to death
and plunder.

The following morning Menac stood in a secluded
spot, at some distance from the encampment, in
earnest conversation with a young warrior of a

bold and prepossessing appearance, whose hand was twisted in the mane of a fiery steed.

" You know the white trader?" said she.

" Yes, he gave me a blanket once."

" Was that all?"

" The first time that I went to hunt he filled my horn with powder, and promised me good luck."

" Think once more. You owe a larger debt than either of those to the white trader."

" When my father was killed by the Sioux, and I was badly wounded, none of the Omawhaws took pity on me, for there was a scarcity in the village. You took me into your wigwam, cured my wounds, and fed me with the white man's provisions."

" You owe him your life."

" I owe it to you."

" To us both."

" I am willing to pay the debt. I have often said that I would die for the New Moon, and I am not unfriendly to the trader; I have eaten his bread."

" You can be secret?"

" The serpent, which has no voice, is not more secret than I."

" Go to the white trader. Let none see you depart—let none but him see you at the principal village of the Omawhaws. Tell him that Menac sent you—that she, who helped to build up his

fortune, who has for years watched over his safety,
now warns him of danger, and bids him fly to the
settlements of his own people.   Say that the spirit
of my father has whispered in my ear that the
Omawhaws have predicted the death of the trader.
Tell him that I shall never see him again—I
would not condescend to be his wife, or his servant; I would starve rather than eat his bread—
but I should grieve to see the father of my children die the death of a dog, or the pale girl, whom
he has chosen for his wife, suffering the penalty of
his crime.   He knows I would not deceive him.
I have but one tongue—it has always spoken the
truth.   We walked together for years—I have
looked back at my path, and find that it is white.
Bid them fly to the fires of the white people, before another moon shall be seen in the place of that
which is now waning.   And say to Bolingbroke—
to the white trader—that if he feels any gratitude
to her who has more than once been a true friend
in the hour of peril, and now saves him, and his
new wife, from the rage of the Omawhaws, he
will restore her daughter to the arms of its mother.   Let him do this, and Menae will forgive
his faithless treatment of herself, and forget all
her sorrows."

The young Indian bent his head, and listened
attentively, as Menae pronounced these words

with a rapid but distinct utterance. He then said, respectfully,

"It shall be done—though it grieves me to disappoint the Omawhaw warriors of their just vengeance. But the daughter of Blackbird was a mother to me, when I was a sick boy; I will be a son to her now that I am a man. When I had no home, I slept in the white man's house: it shall not be burned over his head."

He loosened his hand from the mane of the young horse, on whose neck he leaned, and the liberated animal dashed away over the plain, snuffing the keen air of the morning, and throwing up the snow with his heels.

"Why turn loose your horse," enquired his companion, "when you have immediate use for his services?"

The Indian smiled, and said, "No man rides on horseback when his business is secret. My own feet will leave no track upon the frozen snow. I have a store of dried meat hidden in the woods, which I can easily find. Farewell. The grayest head among the Omawhaws shall not find my trail, nor discover my errand."

Shortly after this event, the Indians learned, to their great disappointment, that Bolingbroke had suddenly abandoned the village, with all his property, and announced his intention to return no more; but they never discovered the cause of his abrupt departure. On the next visit of the other traders to St. Louis, the daughter of Menac was placed under their charge, to be delivered to her mother, who received her child with the joy of one who had mourned over a first born. She lived afterwards in retirement, seldom appearing at the festivals of the nation, and observing the decent gravity of a widowed matron—carefully bringing up her children after the fashion of her own people, and continually advising them to avoid the society, the customs, and the vices, of the whites.

THE END.

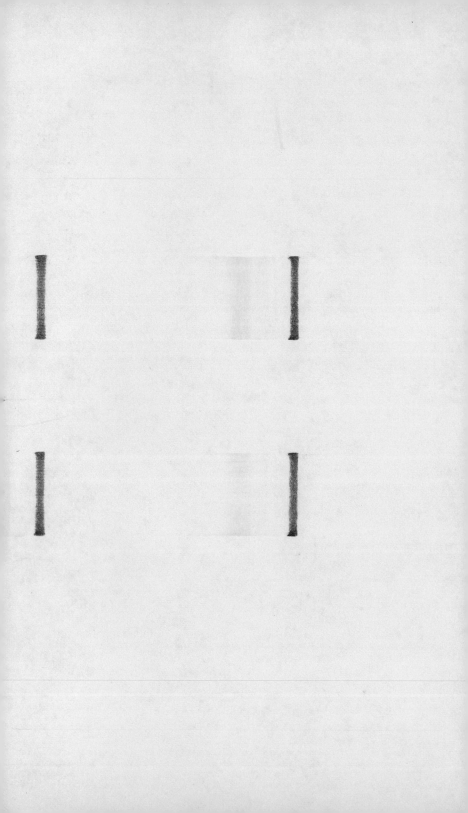